**Sarah found h̶** 
**Kane.**

He had beautiful ... 
capable hands, that would keep ... 
woman—safe. She felt heat rising to her cheeks 
at the thought.

'It must be tough for you,' she said, 'bringing 
up a three-year-old daughter alone.' Was little 
Bambi happy? The poor thing needed a 
mother. A warm, secure family life...

'I manage. And will go on managing!'

**Dear Reader**

Welcome to another title in our FAMILY TIES mini-series! Family...what does it mean to you? The trials and pleasures of children and grandchildren? Loving parents? Brothers and sisters? Whatever it means, you'll enjoy these heartwarming love-stories in which you can meet some fascinating members of our heroes' and heroines' families. And after you've enjoyed this story don't forget to look out for the next FAMILY TIES book, HEARTLESS PURSUIT, by Jessica Steele, next month!

*The Editor*

**Elizabeth Duke** was brought up in the foothills of Adelaide, South Australia, but has lived in Melbourne ever since her marriage to husband John. She trained as a librarian and has worked in various libraries over the years. These days she only works one day a week, as a medical librarian, which gives her time to do what she loves doing most—writing. She also enjoys researching her books and travelling with her husband in Australia and overseas. Their two grown-up children are now married.

# MAKE-BELIEVE FAMILY

BY
**ELIZABETH DUKE**

**MILLS & BOON**

*All the characters in this book have no existence outside the imagination of the author, and have no relation whatsoever to anyone bearing the same name or names. They are not even distantly inspired by any individual known or unknown to the author, and all the incidents are pure invention.*

*MILLS & BOON and the Rose Device
are trademarks of the publisher.
Harlequin Mills & Boon Limited,
Eton House, 18-24 Paradise Road, Richmond, Surrey TW9 1SR
This edition published by arrangement with
Harlequin Enterprises B.V.*

© Elizabeth Duke 1995

ISBN 0 263 79075 4

*Set in Times Roman 10 on 10½ pt.
01-9508-65450 C1*

*Made and printed in Great Britain*

# CHAPTER ONE

'HELP me! Stop! Please...help me!'

Sarah jammed her foot on the brakes as a young woman, waving her arms wildly, leapt from the kerb almost into the path of her car. Pulling to a halt, she wound down her window.

'What is it? What's wrong?' There was parkland alongside the road. Could someone have attacked or robbed the woman as she was taking a walk in the park?

'You're a nurse! Thank God!' cried the woman, catching sight of Sarah's white uniform. 'It's my—my little girl. She's fallen off a swing. She's not moving!'

'Where is she?' Sarah was already out of the car. 'Have you moved her at all?' she asked, breaking into a run as the young woman made a dive for the trees, pointing to a group of yellow-painted swings and slides and monkey-bars.

'I—I didn't dare,' the distraught woman gasped over her shoulder. 'I was scared to touch her. Except to check that she was still breathing. I—I didn't know what to do. She's just lying in the grass.'

'You did the right thing.' Sarah felt a twinge of anxiety. Was the child still unconscious? How badly injured *was* she? 'How long ago did it happen?' she called after her, wondering with a sense of foreboding how long the child had been unconscious.

'A—a minute or two. I ran straight to the road.' The words tumbled out as the young mother ran, scattering leaves and twigs in her path. 'If you hadn't come along, I was going to run to the hospital for help. I—I knew it was next to the park. N-not that I wanted to leave Bambi...' She threw a worried glance behind. '*He'll* say I should have stayed with her!'

5

Sarah caught a flare of fear in the girl's eyes. Who was '*he*', that he could arouse such dread in the poor thing when she was already worried enough about her child? Her husband, presumably.

'But what else could I do?' moaned the girl. 'There was nobody around. Nobody!'

'She'll be all right,' Sarah assured her with more conviction than she felt, not wanting a hysterical mother on her hands as well as an injured child. 'I'm a paediatric nurse at the hospital. Sarah Vane,' she gasped out as she ran.

Next moment she was bending over the small bundle in the grass, her heart leaping to her mouth as she saw how small, how lifeless the little girl looked. She lay ominously still, a deathly pallor showing through the strands of fine dark hair spread across her face. The child's mother had had the foresight to spread a jacket over her for warmth, though, mercifully for Sydney at this time of year, the August afternoon was far from cold.

As Sarah touched the child gently, checking her with the utmost care, she said, 'We'll need an ambulance. I don't want to risk further injury by lifting her and carrying her to the car.'

The young woman made a whimpering sound. She was shaking all over, her pale blue eyes stricken, her fingers clawing at her brown curls in agitation. 'Is she going to be all right? Is she?' She choked back a sob. 'If she d-dies he—he'll kill me!'

Sarah's eyes widened, partly in shock—what kind of monster must the girl's husband be if that was the reaction she expected from him?—and partly in sympathy for the young mother's plight.

'You mustn't blame yourself,' she soothed. 'Accidents happen, unfortunately. She's not going to die,' she assured the girl, in the crisp, calm way she'd assured many other parents during the years she'd been a nurse. 'I expect she'll regain consciousness any second. She may only have a mild concussion. I don't see any evidence of other injury, any fractures or bleeding, but we'd be wise not to move her...just in case.' Just in case *what*, she refrained from spelling out. 'Best to wait for a stretcher...'

As the young mother squeezed her hands in anguish, Sarah said quickly, 'Look, I'll stay here with her if you feel you can drive my car to the hospital. Drive into the emergency bay. It'll be quicker than going on foot. Do you feel up to driving?' she asked in sudden doubt.

'I—I think so.' The girl gulped. 'But I won't need to take your car. I can take my own... It's just over there. I—I was in such a panic I just rushed for the road,' she admitted, flushing, 'hoping someone would come along and help me.' As she stepped back she gave a tiny gasp. 'Oh, no, I completely forgot! There's a *phone* in the car!'

She spun round, moaning over her shoulder, 'You must think I'm such a fool! I could have called an ambulance from the start. I—I was in such a p-panic, I didn't think!'

Sarah gave a bemused shake of her head as the girl stumbled away. Not remembering the mobile phone had wasted precious minutes. Still, the poor thing was undoubtedly in shock.

She looked very young, Sarah thought, barely more than nineteen or twenty. Hardly old enough to be married, let alone to have a child this age... She stroked the hair back from the child's pale face. How old *was* the little girl? she wondered idly. Three, maybe?

Glancing round, she caught a glimpse of the other car for the first time as the young mother reached the spot where she'd parked it under a clump of gum-trees. A Mercedes. A brand-new one, by the look of it, silvery-grey paintwork gleaming in the winter sunlight.

The girl looked too young, too unsophisticated to own such a car, Sarah thought... An expensive luxury car, complete with mobile phone. Probably it was her husband's car and she'd just borrowed it for the day, and that was why she'd forgotten it had a mobile phone.

The poor girl seemed totally in awe of her husband, terrified of his reaction, Sarah mused, wondering what kind of man he must be to make his young wife so fearful of him.

The girl was back within seconds, hovering anxiously over her. 'They're sending an ambulance straight away.' Relief throbbed through her voice. 'Listen!' Her head whipped round. 'I can hear a siren already!'

'Good.' Glancing up, Sarah smiled encouragement. 'Children are very resilient,' she assured the trembling girl.

'You've been awfully kind.' Tears gushed from the girl's eyes. 'It's all my fault!' she burst out. 'I should never have let her go on that swing. I should never have pushed her so high! That's what *he'll* say, and he—he'll be right!' Burying her face in her hands, she broke into choking sobs.

'Please...try to keep calm.' The poor girl seemed even more afraid of the father's reaction, Sarah thought, with a surge of resentment towards the man, than of the possible fate of her child. Unless it was simply her way of dealing with the crisis. People reacted to shock in different ways. By concentrating on the father's anger, the young mother could be trying to blot out an even greater fear, a fear too frightening to contemplate.

'You didn't do it deliberately,' Sarah reminded her firmly. 'And I'm sure your husband won't——'

'He—he's not my husband!'

'Oh.' Sarah let that sink in, only noticing then, as she flicked a glance upward, that the girl wasn't wearing a wedding-ring. So the couple weren't married. Well, that wasn't so unusual these days.

'He—he never did trust me with her!' the girl gulped out between sobs. 'He was always expecting something to happen, warning me to be careful, and now—and now...'

'It was an *accident*,' Sarah stressed. What a monster the child's father sounded! The poor girl was scared witless. 'The main thing is, you didn't move her. You kept your head ... that's not easy in a crisis.'

'*He* won't think so... even if she does fully recover.' The girl's voice was bitter through her tears. 'You— you'd think she was made of crystal, the way he fusses and frets over her, and all the instructions he leaves with me, and the number of times a day he rings up from work. Let alone the grilling I get when he gets home. And I *know* he gets the housekeeper to spy on me!'

*Housekeeper*? Sarah frowned up at the pale, ravaged face. This unassuming young girl had a *housekeeper*? 'You ... *are* the child's mother?' she asked slowly, more to clarify the matter than anything—never really doubting for a moment, with the girl in such a state over the child, that she could be anything else.

The girl stared at her. 'Gosh, did you think...?' She shook her head. 'Heavens, no. I'm just l-looking after her. I'm her n-nanny. Beth Newbold. I—I've only been with her for three weeks. That's *his* car over there... He insists I drive it when I take Bambi out. He doesn't think my Mini is safe enough.'

'Oh.' Sarah nodded, her eyes thoughtful. Before she could comment further, two things happened: the child gave a low moan, and the ambulance, siren wailing, swung into the park, pulling up near the Mercedes at the edge of the playground. Sarah smiled up at Beth Newbold. 'Everything will be all right now,' she said, and she bent over the child, hiding her own relief.

Sarah followed the ambulance and the Mercedes, with a pale-faced Beth at the wheel, to the hospital, and, after parking her car in the staff car-park, hastened into the emergency department as she had promised Beth she would, only pausing at the desk to put a call through to the paediatric ward, where she was due to go on duty at three, only minutes away.

'Paula, I'll be a few minutes late. I'm down in Casualty with a child who's fallen off a swing. I want to make sure she's all right before I come up. OK?'

'Sure. It's not too frantic up here, luckily. Come up when you're ready. I'll know where you are if I need you.'

'Thanks.'

She found Beth in X-ray, hovering inside the doorway of one of the cubicles. The girl's face brightened as she turned and saw her. She gave a shaky smile and stepped over to grasp Sarah's arm.

'They want to X-ray her skull,' she said with a shudder. 'But at least she's conscious now. Not that she's spoken or anything. But she never does...much.' She stifled a sigh. 'Not to anyone. Not even to me.'

Sarah pursed her lips, wondering how much the father's overbearing attitude had to do with the little girl's timidity.

'Sarah, thanks for coming.' Beth's fingers clung to Sarah's arm. 'You've been so good.'

'I'm glad I was able to help. Beth...have you told the sister-in-charge that you're not the child's mother? Have they contacted her parents yet? Her father?' Beth had made no mention of a mother, but that could have been because she wasn't so in awe of the wife as she was of the husband. What kind of wife, Sarah paused to wonder, employed a nanny *and* a housekeeper? A full-time career woman who was seldom at home? Or maybe a spoilt, pampered young wife, lucky enough to have a husband who could afford such luxuries?

Beth's small white teeth tugged at her lip. 'There hasn't been time to make a call. They rushed her straight in here. And—and there's only him. Bambi's father,' she told Sarah in a hushed voice. 'He's never mentioned Bambi's mother. Nobody has. All they've said is that Bambi has no mother.' She heaved a sigh. 'He...won't be in his office. He's flown to Canberra for the day. On business.'

So...no mother. Divorced, more than likely. Mmm... That figures, Sarah thought uncharitably. By the sound of him, a woman would need to be a saint to put up with him! But how could such an ogre have won custody of the child? Because *he* had the money, the power and the influence, no doubt, she concluded cynically.

But he was still the child's father. 'Is there any way we can get in touch with him?' she asked Beth gently. 'He should be here.' Glancing past Beth, she could see the radiologist conferring with the young doctor and the nurse who were attending Bambi.

'You think she might...need an operation?' Beth's eyes widened in panic. 'Or be...you know? Affected by the fall?'

'Beth, he's the child's father... He should be here with her, whether she's OK or not. Or at least be told. Can you find a way to contact him?'

Beth sighed. 'Y-yes. I think so. He always leaves his number, wherever he is. Will—will you call for me?' she begged. 'His name is...K-Kane Brody.'

'If you like. You have his number?'

As the girl fumbled in her purse the young doctor joined them, his nurse hovering behind.

'There's no sign of a fracture,' he told Beth, and Beth clasped Sarah's arm in relief. 'She appears to be suffering a mild concussion, that's all. You're the little girl's mother?' he asked her.

Beth shook her head, and Sarah said quickly, 'She's Bambi's nanny, Beth Newbold. I was just about to call the father for her. He's not in town—he's in Canberra for the day. Beth says there is no mother.'

'Try to get on to him, will you? I'd like to admit Bambi overnight for observation...just as a precaution,' the doctor assured Beth quickly, as he noted her agitation. 'Sarah, better still, Sister Elliott here can make the call; it's not your job. You must be due to go on duty upstairs, aren't you?'

Sarah nodded. 'I've let them know. It's all right.' But she did as he suggested and handed over Beth's slip of paper.

'In the meantime——' the doctor turned back to Beth '—we'll need to know a few things about your young charge. You won't mind answering a few questions, will you, before her father arrives? Once we have the details we need, we'll find a bed for her in the children's ward. Just wait here for a moment, will you? I'll be right back. Don't worry about Bambi. She's sleeping peacefully now.'

The moment he left, Beth's slight body seemed to shrivel. 'They want to *admit* her?' she whispered. 'He—he'll never forgive me! He'll kick me out, I know he will.'

Sarah stared at her. Surely, she thought in secret outrage, the poor girl couldn't be expecting that monster to *dismiss* her. It would be grossly unfair! Silently cursing the child's high-handed parent, she gave Beth's arm a squeeze. 'It'll be OK, Beth. They're only admitting her overnight—it's usual procedure when someone's been unconscious. It sounds as if Bambi's going to be just fine. And I'll be able to keep an eye on her personally when they bring her up to the children's ward.'

'Oh, Sarah, I don't know what I would have done without you!' Beth's eyes filled with tears. 'Thanks for—for everything. You've been just great. I—I'm sorry if I've held you up.'

'You haven't. See you later!'

Sarah looked up from the patient she was tending to see Bambi being wheeled into the ward. Beth was following behind, nervously twisting her hands, though she brightened when she saw Sarah.

Sarah gave her a smile and looked down at the small child on the trolley. Two huge brown eyes in a small pale face gazed up at her.

'Hello, Bambi.' Sarah bent over her. 'I'm Sister Vane—Sarah. Your nurse. Feeling a little better?'

The child didn't respond. Not even a nod. She just stared, wide-eyed and unblinking, at Sarah.

'She's very shy,' Beth whispered. 'She's always like this.'

'It's all strange to her.' Sarah smiled down at Bambi. 'It's all right, Bambi. You're in the children's ward now. There are other children here too,' she told her.

As the orderly lifted the child from the trolley and transferred her to a bed with a screen on one side to cut out the bright light from the window, Sarah asked Beth quickly, 'Did they get on to her father? Is he on his way?'

Beth nodded, a shiver quivering through her. 'Yes, he should be here any minute. Sister Elliott spoke to him.' She sounded relieved that someone else had taken on the task of breaking the news to him. 'He said he'd be on the next plane. That was over an hour ago.'

Sarah turned back to the bed, talking gently as she tucked in the blankets and brushed strands of dark hair from the child's pale face. 'Your daddy will be here to see you any time now, Bambi. And Beth is here too. And I know something else you might like.'

She plucked a soft teddy bear from the shelf behind, one of the toys they kept handy in the ward for their young patients.

To her consternation, the child's brown eyes filled with tears. As Sarah held the toy out to her, instead of accepting it, the little girl squeezed her eyes shut and turned her head away.

'I suppose you'd rather have one of your own toys,' Sarah said perceptively. 'Beth, when her father comes, maybe you could slip home and fetch a few of her favourites. Or would you have any of her toys in the car?'

Beth flushed. 'I—I didn't think to take any with us when we drove to the playground. There's only her old blanket. She drags it around wherever she goes. She even takes it to bed with her. Her father would have a fit if I brought that in. It's stained and—and frayed. He hates it!'

'I think she should have it. She needs something familiar right now. Never mind what it looks like. Would you mind...?'

'OK.' Beth glanced down at Bambi, who was staring solemnly up at her. 'I'll be right back, love, with your blanket. Won't be long. You'll be fine with Sarah.' As she hurried across the ward to the door she faltered, and then shrank back.

'Where the hell do you think you're going?' a harsh voice rasped. 'Running away so you won't have to face the music?'

Sarah looked up, frowning, as a broad-shouldered man in a dark business suit strode into the ward, leaving Beth cowering, frozen, against the wall. The roomy four-bed ward seemed suddenly to shrink, as much from the man's dynamic presence as his six-foot-plus frame.

Sarah hastened across the ward to confront him. 'Would you mind keeping your voice down?' she cautioned, coming to a halt in front of him—and feeling rather as if she had crashed straight into a stone wall, such was the impact of coming face to face with the man. It was the oddest feeling. Power—or was it the man's fury?—flowed from him in waves, leaving her quite shaken for a second. No wonder poor Beth was so much in awe of him!

'Where is she?' he rapped out, ignoring her plea to keep his voice down. Before Sarah could answer, he caught sight of his daughter, and Sarah had to leap aside to avoid being knocked down in his rush to reach her bedside.

'Bambi, honey...are you all right?'

The change in his voice, from that harsh, angry rasp to the softest velvet, was as stunning as everything else about him. Sarah dragged her gaze away from him with an effort, and gave Beth, still standing stricken near the doorway, a quick nod. Even if Bambi had no need of her frayed old blanket right now, while her father was here, she was bound to want it later, after he had gone.

'Daddy's here, baby. You're all right now.' The man's deep voice, muted as it was, was still clearly audible across the room. 'Nothing else is going to happen to you... I promise.' As Sarah glanced round she saw him drop into a chair beside the bed and reach out to stroke the child's pale face. Deciding to leave them alone for the moment, she busied herself with the other patients in the room. There were only two other children in the ward at present: a five-year-old boy recovering from a tonsillectomy and an eight-year-old girl being observed overnight for possible appendicitis.

By the time Beth crept back into the ward with the child's frayed blanket Bambi was sleeping peacefully, her father still by her side, his hand resting on his daughter's smooth brow. But when he glanced up and saw Beth, he drew back his hand and was out of his chair and across the ward in a couple of angry strides.

'How could you let this happen?' He looked ready to grab her by the throat and wring her neck. 'You were meant to be taking care of her! Can't I trust anybody to look after my child? Am I fated never to find a competent nanny for my daughter?'

As Beth wilted under his fury, Sarah, who had been reading a story to the five-year-old in the next bed, jumped to her feet and hurried across the room.

'Would you mind stepping out into the corridor?' Her face was sternly implacable as she steered them both out. 'You'll wake Bambi and disturb the other children.'

'I'm lucky to have a child to wake!' snapped the child's father. 'I *warned* the girl to be careful around swings. For pity's sake, the child's only three years old!'

No matter how much she might secretly agree with him—pushing the child so high that she was able to fall off and hurt herself had been a foolishly dangerous thing to do—Sarah had no intention, for Beth's sake, of stirring him further. He might show at least some feeling for the girl. As if Beth didn't feel bad enough already!

'Accidents happen, Mr Brody.' She kept her tone clipped, severe. 'And would you mind keeping your voice down? This is a hospital, remember. There are sick people here.'

His eyes—greenish eyes, she noted, flecked with grey—flickered under her disapproving gaze, as if he were seeing her for the first time. With a shrug, he snapped his gaze away, jerking his head round to face Beth.

'You can go home. I'm here to look after her now. Drop my car off, collect your things, and then leave. I'll send your cheque in the post.'

Beth caught her breath. 'You mean——?'

'I mean I won't be needing your services any longer,' he spelt out without pity.

Tears sprang to Beth's eyes. She bit her lip, and glanced down at the frayed blanket in her hand. 'I—I brought this in for Bambi.' Hands shaking, she held it out to him.

'That old thing!' Kane Brody gave a snort of disgust. 'I thought I told you to get rid of it. Where's that new doll I bought her? Or *any* of the dolls or toys that I've bought her recently? Any one of them must be a vast improvement on that old rag!'

'She—she...' Exposed to his fury, Beth didn't seem capable of getting a word out.

Sarah intervened swiftly, her voice calm but firm. 'Sometimes a child gets attached to something simply because it's old and familiar. Even an old blanket can be a big comfort to a child. Hence the term comfort-blanket,' she explained patiently.

She saw a tiny light flicker in his eyes. Anger, most likely, at her impudence. Being spoken to in that patronising way! That glint in his eyes was hardly likely to be...contrition. A man like Kane Brody, suffering contrition? Involuntarily, her lip quivered. She flushed. Curse her wretched sense of humour! It had a habit of flaring to life at the most inopportune times.

She saw him still watching her, and sobered instantly. This was no laughing matter. Least of all to poor Beth.

'Let me give it to Bambi,' she said steadily, her gaze holding his as she took the old blanket from Beth's trembling fingers. 'Unless you would prefer to?' she asked impassively, giving him the choice. It was a ploy she used with children. Offering a choice.

For a moment longer their eyes remained locked, almost in a silent battle of wills. She had a feeling that this man didn't lose many battles in his life. But then, she thought, rallying, neither did she.

'I'll give it to her,' he said at length, gruffly, and Sarah released her breath—which she hadn't even realised she was holding.

She gave him a sudden smile. 'I'm sure she'll be grateful,' she said, and immediately found her gaze locked to his again, only this time not in battle. He looked faintly startled.

She swallowed, thrown off balance for a second. Surely a simple smile couldn't have pierced this man's thick armour! But when, in the blink of an eye, his gaze flicked coldly away, his mouth tightening at the same time, she knew she must have imagined it. If anything had startled him, it was more likely the realisation that he had given in to her. Given in to a mere woman! It must have come as quite a shock to him!

'I—I'll be off then,' Beth whispered, addressing Sarah, not Kane Brody. He had already dismissed her. From his mind—and from his employ.

'Bambi will be all right, Beth. Try not to blame yourself too much. Accidents can happen so suddenly, in the blink of an eye,' Sarah said pointedly, for Kane Brody's benefit. The girl's carelessness might have been responsible for what had happened in the first place, but she had acted promptly and responsibly and hadn't lost her head—apart from forgetting the mobile phone. 'You were quite right not attempting to move her yourself.'

'Coping with emergencies was part of my training,' Beth said gratefully—at the same time making a point of her own, reminding her employer that she had been well trained for her job. But it was lost on Kane Brody. He was already striding back into the ward, the worn blanket dangling from his fingers.

When Sarah returned to the ward a few minutes later, Bambi was clutching the blanket tightly, and there was even a faint tinge of colour in her face. The eyes that looked up at Sarah this time, though still wide, still un-blinking, held a spark of something, a clinging softness that hadn't been there before. Was she, Sarah wondered with a faint jolt, saying a silent thank-you for the blanket?

She smiled down at the child and saw the tiny rosebud mouth stir faintly at the edges. Almost a smile! Sarah felt a rush of warmth inside.

Kane Brody was sitting in a chair beside the bed. He looked up at her as she turned to face him, a hint of a frown creasing his brow as he saw her open her mouth to speak.

It's all right, Sarah's eyes told him coolly as she in-terpreted the warning frown. I'm not about to plead for Beth in front of Bambi. I'm not that silly.

'I'll stay with Bambi, Mr Body,' she offered briskly, 'if you'd like to slip down to the canteen for some coffee or a bite to eat.' He'd obviously driven straight to the hospital from the airport after, presumably, a long working day in Canberra, with no doubt a rushed lunch or no lunch at all. He looked as if he could do with some refreshment. Tufts of brown hair flopped over his brow, his hard square-jawed face was lined with fatigue, and he'd undone the top button of his white shirt and his loosened tie was askew.

'Later, maybe.' There was no softening in his tone. The coldness, the hardness were still there, though at least he'd toned down the volume. Maybe he didn't ap-preciate nurses—*women*—fussing over him. Maybe he had something against women, period—a chip on his shoulder as a result, perhaps, of his ill-fated marriage. Those lines around his mouth... There was cynicism there as well as the tiredness and strain. She found herself wondering again about his marriage. Had his wife walked out on *him*? Or had he left *her*? If she had left him, why hadn't she taken Bambi with her? Had he prevented her? It was all very puzzling.

She shrugged, resolving to call down to the kitchen staff to send up some coffee and sandwiches for him. Excusing herself, she moved over to check on the other children. The boy was sound asleep and the girl with the suspect appendix had her mother and baby sister with her. After satisfying herself that they were both comfortable, she headed for the door. 'I'll be in the nurses' station outside if you need me, Mr Brody,' she said, pausing as she passed by his daughter's bed. 'I'll be back shortly to check on Bambi.'

Kane Brody nodded, barely even glancing at her.

Not long afterwards Dr Graham, the paediatrician, arrived, and Paula, the other nursing sister on duty, accompanied him on his rounds. After the doctor had gone, Paula burst into the nurses' station and grabbed Sarah's arm.

'Do you know who that is in there?' she asked, her hazel eyes dancing with excitement as she pointed towards the ward.

'You mean ... the man with Bambi? Bambi's father?'

'Of course I mean him! Who else?'

Grinning, Sarah shook her head. A handsome face or a sexy hunk always had this effect on Paula. 'All I know is that his name's Kane Brody,' she said with feigned indifference. 'And he can be very fierce, so I wouldn't——'

'Oh, Sarah, don't be silly. Kane Brody's quite out of my league.' Paula heaved a sigh. 'You mean—you honestly don't know who he is?'

'Sorry, I——'

'I don't believe it! Don't you ever read the papers?'

'The papers?' Was Kane Brody somebody famous? She'd never heard of him! 'I don't really study the gossip columns,' she confessed.

'Not the gossip columns, silly. The business section. There was a write-up on him only last week.'

'Oh. The business section.' Sarah pulled a face. 'I'm not really into big business either.' But she *was* curious about Kane Brody. 'So? Who is he?'

'You've never heard of Kane Brody, the multimillion-aire merchant banker? He's only one of the top cor-porate advisers in Australia!' Paula's hazel eyes glinted in triumph. 'The man's been involved in some amazing business deals. He's made millions!'

'At the expense of his child, no doubt,' Sarah mut-tered sourly, thinking of poor little Bambi, left at home alone with her nannies.

'Sarah, he's devoted to his daughter—that's common knowledge,' Paula asserted. She added dreamily, 'He's got the lot, my father says. Blue-chip client list. Government contacts. A reputation for getting things done. To say nothing of flair, good looks, and money laid-on. Dad says it's no wonder everyone's clamouring for his services.' She gave a lewd chuckle. 'I bet there are heaps of women clamouring for his services too—if you know what I mean! Sarah, there was a photograph of him with the write-up...surely you saw it? How could you *not* have noticed? He's such a spunk!'

'A spunk?' That was hardly how Sarah would have described Kane Brody. Certainly, the man had presence. He made an impact on people—a powerful impact. She'd felt it herself. But he was far too overbearing, too abrasive, too insensitive in her opinion, ever to earn the label 'spunky'!

'What did the article say about him?' she asked, interested despite herself.

'Oh, it was all about his business deals and his law reform plans, nothing personal. That's the way he likes it, apparently. My father's met him a few times—Kane Brody has directorships on a number of company boards, including my dad's. Dad says he's a terribly private person—not the type to talk about himself or make idle chit-chat, even when they meet outside the office or at social functions. So I guess he'd hardly open up to reporters. Not about his private life, I mean. He's ready enough to talk business any time. But I do know something,' she confided, leaning closer.

'He's divorced,' Sarah provided with a wry smile.

Paula blinked at her. 'Divorced? Where in the world did you get that idea? He's a widower. His wife died nearly two years ago. Sarah, that makes him *very* eligible.' She sighed elaborately. 'At least in certain lucky circles. I mean, with a three-year-old child—a poor motherless daughter—he *must* be on the lookout for another wife!'

Sarah stared at her, only the first part sinking in. 'His wife *died*?' That, she guessed could explain a lot. The man's over-protectiveness, his intense concern for his child, the need for a nanny and a housekeeper. Even Bambi's shyness, the big sad eyes. Her heart went out to the child. And to Kane Brody too—the grieving husband, the father left behind, still too anguished after nearly two years to talk about the wife he'd lost.

He wouldn't be the type of man to confide easily in people, Sarah suspected—let alone in his child's nanny. And Beth, being so much in awe of him, wouldn't be the type to force confidences from him . . . or even from his housekeeper.

Poor Beth. Kane Brody would only have had to say, 'Bambi's mother is not to be mentioned,' and she wouldn't have. She wouldn't have dared.

'His wife was killed in a car accident,' Paula went on, glancing round to make sure no one could hear them. 'Apparently her car hit a power-pole after running off the road, and she was killed instantly. They say she was a raving beauty. Italian. It was in the papers at the time.

Just a brief report. As I said, Kane Brody avoids personal publicity like the plague. Always has.'

Sarah pursed her lips, not commenting for a moment. What a terrible thing. To have his wife snatched from him so tragically, in a shocking instant . . . leaving him to bring up his small daughter alone. Terrible for him and for Bambi. No wonder his daughter was so precious to him. No wonder he worried so much about her.

'Bambi's nearly four now, according to her chart,' she mused aloud, 'so she must have been only two at the time.' Did the child still remember her mother? Still pine for her? Had her father, young as she had been at the time of the accident, told her the truth—that her mother was dead, gone from her life forever—and tried to comfort her? Or had he put it off, wanting to protect her from the pain and grief he must have been feeling himself, thinking it better to wait until she was old enough to understand properly?

Sarah chewed on her lip. Parents often did try to shield their children that way. And their motives were understandable. But, from her experience with grieving children, it was a mistake, she had found, to hold back the truth. Evading it, keeping the true facts from a child, even a child as young as Bambi, often made it even harder for the child to accept the truth when it did finally hear it.

'He's not quite what I expected,' Paula admitted with a sigh. 'Of course, it must have come as a shock to him, hearing that his daughter had been rushed to hospital with a head injury. But . . .' She hesitated, casting around for an explanation for her disappointment.

'He didn't exactly set out to . . . charm you?' Sarah ventured, her blue eyes dancing.

Paula grimaced. 'No . . . He just scowled at me. He wanted to know where *you* were. He said he wanted *you* to take care of his child—just you. I tried to explain to him that we both have several patients under our care, and we can't always be in two places at once. But that wouldn't do for Kane Brody. He made Dr Graham promise that whenever you were on duty *you* would be the one primarily responsible for Bambi's care. The arrogance of the man!'

'Not quite the charming spunk you thought?' teased Sarah, flushing faintly at the thought of Kane Brody making such a demand. It came as a surprise. He hadn't shown any particular goodwill towards her in her presence.

Paula shrugged. 'I still think he's spunky. A real hunk. But he'd be far too hard to handle, in my opinion. He's one of those larger-than-life types. You'd have to be on your toes the whole time. I prefer simpler, more amiable guys. Like my Sam. Someone who really appreciates a girl.' She tossed her curly head. 'I'd be a fool to let Sam out of my clutches.'

'You would, indeed,' said Sarah, and hid a sigh. There was no man in her life...nor was there ever likely to be. Not on a permanent basis, at any rate. A long, happy family life was for other women. Not for Sarah Vane. David had shown her that, bowing out of her life the day he proposed marriage to her, after she'd told him she couldn't have children.

No use crying about it. She'd made her plans for the future, exciting plans too, and she was going to stick to them. Come what may.

# CHAPTER TWO

KANE BRODY was still at Bambi's bedside when the children's evening meals were brought in. Sarah noted that Bambi ate very little, even with her father's help.

'Don't worry too much,' she said as she moved the tray aside. 'She'd probably rather sleep.'

'She never eats much,' Kane Brody growled. 'The doctors I've seen say there's nothing wrong with her.' He gave a disbelieving grunt. 'She hardly eats enough to keep a bird alive.'

'Best not to force her,' Sarah said lightly. 'You could try...' She hesitated. Telling Kane Brody what to do or not do was fraught with pitfalls. He hadn't asked for her advice! Besides, discussing Bambi's eating habits in front of the child wasn't a good idea. 'Maybe we could talk about it later,' she suggested, adopting her brisk nurse's tone to hide a sudden quickening of her heartbeat. The thought of spending more time with Kane Brody gave her a whole mixture of churned-up feelings inside. Excitement, apprehension, exhilaration, danger. Like playing with fire.

'Excuse me...' She backed away before he could accept or refuse her offer. 'I must check the children in the next ward.'

When she came back to settle Bambi and the other two children down for the night, she was surprised to see that Kane Brody was still there. Fathers normally didn't stay long with their children—or they were unable to, for various reasons. But of course Bambi was different, a special case. She didn't have a mother to stay with her, and her nanny had been dismissed.

Was Kane Brody as attentive and caring as this at normal times? she found herself pondering. Or did the demands of his high-profile job keep him away from his daughter for much of the time? Nannies, house-keepers ... Did he rely on them, perhaps, *too much*?

Well, he has no nanny to rely on now! she thought with a rueful sigh, thinking of poor Beth.

'You should go home now, and rest yourself,' she heard herself telling him, noting the dark smudges under his eyes and the deepening lines round his mouth. 'And you should eat something too. You haven't taken a break since you've been here.'

'Do you fuss like this over all the parents who stay with their children?' he asked irritably. 'You sent for some coffee and sandwiches for me earlier, remember? So I'm not exactly starving. Nor am I ready to fall into bed just yet,' he growled, watching her as she moved over to close the slatted blinds covering the windows.

She turned with a faint smile. No, he didn't look the type who would wilt under pressure, no matter how tired and hungry he was. He would have the energy of ten men, she didn't doubt.

He eyed her narrowly, speculatively. 'You've been on the go yourself all the time I've been here,' he drawled. 'Don't *you* ever take a break?'

'I'm about to take my tea-break now, as a matter of fact.' A half-hour break before working on until eleven. 'Paula—Sister Marks—will watch over Bambi.'

'You take your meals in the hospital canteen?' he asked, and when she nodded, wondering why he would care where she ate or what she did in her spare time, he added, surprising her further, 'I might see you down there. You're right ... I should eat. If I have a meal here at the hospital, I can pop up here again afterwards and make sure Bambi's settled down for the night before I go home.'

It wasn't exactly an invitation to join her for dinner, but it came close. For some reason Sarah's pulse-rate quickened at the thought of getting together with him over a meal—at the thought of him *wanting* her company. He hadn't struck her as being the sociable type—let alone being sociable with his child's nurse. With nurses or nannies or anybody!

Then she remembered her tentative offer earlier to discuss Bambi's eating habits. Was that what he had in mind? Whatever it was, he would be thinking of Bambi, wanting to help *her*. Maybe he had some special instructions for her...to make sure his daughter was getting the very best of care. He idolised his little girl, obviously. And worried about her—too much, perhaps. If what Beth had told her was true, he believed in wrapping his child in cotton wool. If he kept on that way he could end up stifling her independence, repressing her development, and end up with a helpless, dependent child who couldn't think or act for herself.

Would she be brave enough to tell him so?

'Why don't you go down now?' she suggested. He would hardly want to be seen walking down to the canteen with one of the nurses! It might lead to speculation. 'I'll just finish up here. Sister Marks will keep an eye on Bambi while I'm at tea. And you won't need to worry about Bambi overnight...I'll be here until eleven, and then the night staff come on. They're wonderful with the children and will keep your daughter under close observation all night. We've all been trained in paediatric nursing,' she assured him.

He rose from his chair, and muttered in an undertone so that his daughter couldn't overhear, 'Bambi tends to be afraid of the dark.'

'Please, don't worry. We keep soft lights on all night in the wards. And the children are checked regularly. If they wake up, or seem disturbed in any way, a nurse will stay with them. Bambi will be checked each half-hour, awake or asleep.'

'It's all strange to her here,' he said, and as she glanced up and caught his gaze she noted bemusedly that his eyes looked grey now, where earlier they had been a distinct green. Eyes that changed with the light. 'She's never been in hospital before,' he stressed.

She flicked a tongue over her lips. 'I know. And I understand. I'll leave you to say goodnight to her...' She gave him a brief smile and moved over to the boy in the next bed. A few minutes later, when she glanced back at Bambi's bed, Kane Brody had gone. Bambi's dark eyes glistened in the dim light. She hadn't made a sound.

When Sarah wandered into the hospital canteen soon afterwards, she saw Kane Brody carrying a tray of food to one of the tables. She gave him a nod as he glanced round and saw her, and after choosing her own meal at the counter took it over to join him.

She found herself hesitating before putting her tray down on his table. Perhaps he hadn't meant...

'Please...sit down,' he invited, and she gave a brief nod and pulled out a chair. 'Bambi's settled down?' he asked as she sat down opposite him. His face was impassive, his eyes unreadable under his dark flickering lashes, but she sensed his concern underneath.

'She's fast asleep,' she assured him. 'She settled down beautifully.' Almost too well. Did the child ever cry? Or complain? Or throw a tantrum? she wondered.

'Is there going to be anyone at home to look after her when she leaves here?' she asked. She was thinking of Beth, no longer there for the child. The poor child needed a regular carer, preferably someone familiar, someone close to the family, to be always there for her.

He frowned, his gaze piercing hers, a faint glitter in the grey-green depths. 'If you have something to say about my treatment of Beth, go ahead... Say it.'

She took a deep breath. Why hold back? He was inviting her to speak up! 'Don't you think you were rather hard on her?' she asked quietly, hoping he would give Beth another chance. 'Couldn't you see that she was distraught? She felt bad enough without you making her feel worse, and humiliating her in front of the nursing staff.'

'She deserved it.' He speared a potato on his fork. 'I put my trust in her. She should have taken more care. Can't a man expect a bit of responsibility from the person he leaves in charge of his child? What kind of incompetent,' he rasped, 'would let a three-year-old swing so high that she could fall off and hurt herself?'

Sarah had no answer to that. But the memory of Beth's distress plucked a further word in the girl's defence. 'Believe me, Mr Kane, Beth has learned her lesson—the hard way. You can be sure she'll take more care around swings in future. She seemed very fond of your daughter. I do wish you would give her just one more chance. Haven't *you* ever made mistakes—and learnt from them?' she challenged.

Immediately she sensed that she had gone too far. His eyes flashed green fire, his mouth hardening under her gaze. As she held her breath, not moving a muscle, steeling herself for what was coming, she was relieved to see the fire fading from his eyes, the lines of weariness in his face seeming suddenly more marked.

'I'll tell her she can come in and say goodbye to Bambi,' he growled, 'but——' his tone was unrelenting '—I won't take her back. My cheque will more than adequately cover her until she finds another post.'

Sarah released her breath slowly. Hardly a backdown...but some slight concession. Perhaps as much as poor Beth deserved. She *had* been in a position of trust.

They bent over their food, eating in silence for a few moments. He was the first to break it.

'I haven't actually thanked *you*.' His eyes, she noted as she glanced up in surprise, were shuttered, his eyelids half drawn. There was no softness there that she could discern. No softness in his voice either. Was he afraid to show any softening of emotion for fear that she might take his remarks personally, and get foolish ideas? *Very* eligible, Paula had called him. Was he wary of women because of that, convinced that they were all after him and that any encouragement from him would have them jumping to all kinds of mistaken conclusions?

Was he, even after nearly two years, still mourning his dead wife?

'Thank me?' she echoed with equal coolness.

'The emergency staff told me what you did for my daughter. And I understand you stayed around until she had been examined and X-rayed, and that it was your calmness that stopped Beth going completely to pieces.' His mouth twisted, as if he expected nothing less of his daughter's ex-nanny.

'There's no need... I just did my job.' Sarah gave a shrug. 'Poor Beth,' she added deliberately, 'was devastated by what happened.'

'Devastated that Bambi was seriously hurt? Or at the thought of facing *me*?' His tone was caustic.

Sarah steeled herself against his scorn. 'But surely one mistake... an *accident*...?'

'An accident that could have had disastrous results,' he grated, unmoved. 'It's not just today. It's other things. Careless, thoughtless things. I've had to be on her back constantly.'

'But surely Beth's credentials——?' Sarah broke off with a sigh, wondering why she was persisting. She clearly wasn't going to make him change his mind. And maybe Beth did have her faults, though she was inclined to believe that even a saint wouldn't be perfect enough for Kane Brody.

'Her credentials?' His lips curled. 'Oh, yes, her credentials, her training, were impeccable. She came highly recommended, no argument. But then so did all the others.'

'*All* the others?' Sarah echoed. How many nannies had the poor child had this past couple of years?

'The nannies we've had to date have either proved unsuitable or left of their own accord.' Kane's mouth thinned in scorn. 'It never ceases to amaze me how easily some women will wilt under pressure.'

Sarah speculated on where the pressure would have come from. From *him*? Bambi didn't strike her as being a difficult or demanding child, and household chores wouldn't have been involved since Kane Brody had a housekeeper. He would not, she imagined wryly, be an easy boss to work for.

Her brow creased in a frown. It was tragic that Bambi was being tossed from one stranger to another, from one short-lived caretaker to another. 'You don't have a woman in the family who could help out?' she ventured. 'An aunt? Bambi's grandparents? A family friend?'

'Not on a permanent basis.' His eyes swivelled to hers. There was speculation in the grey-green depths. Was he looking *at* her, she wondered, feeling vaguely unnerved, or *through* her? 'My mother helps out now and then,' he said after a pause, 'but she's overseas at present on a buying trip. She's a buyer for Grace Brothers.'

Sarah let her gaze flutter away from his, her heart going out to Bambi. Even the child's own grandmother put the demands of her job ahead of her grandchild.

'My mother's not the domestic type.' It was almost as if Kane had read her thoughts. 'She's OK with Bambi in small doses, but it would never work out on a permanent basis. She likes her work too much. And her freedom. And why shouldn't she have her own life?' he said with a shrug. 'Bambi is my responsibility.'

Sarah dug her spoon into her fruit trifle and tried to look non-committal. After all, it was none of her business.

'You have no brothers or sisters?' she asked.

'Only a brother. He's in the diplomatic service, based overseas.'

'What about your... wife's family?'

There was a long, heavy pause. Then, 'What do you know about my wife?' His tone had changed, sharpened.

She swallowed. 'Only what most people know, I guess. That she died in an accident.' Let him think she had read it in the papers. 'I'm sorry,' she said inadequately.

'I prefer not to talk about my wife.' His eyes were hard now, his tone icily implacable. The deep lines round his mouth could have been etched in stone.

'I understand,' she said, her gaze flickering under his. He must have loved his wife very much for it to be so painful still. 'But her family...?' She looked at him enquiringly. Didn't they help out with Bambi?

'They're not here in Australia. They're Italian. They live in Milan.'

'Oh.' She pushed her plate aside and glanced at her watch. 'I must get back.'

'I'll come up with you.' He scraped back his chair. She felt suddenly dwarfed as he stood up, towering over her.

She drew in a deep breath as she turned away, steadying herself before leading the way out. As her legs propelled her forward she forced herself to concentrate her thoughts on the man's daughter, rather than on the man himself.

'Bambi will be fine,' she assured him as they took a lift to the next floor. Poor kid. She had no one else but him now. A part-time father with a demanding, high-profile job that kept him away from her, probably far too much. A father who compensated by being over-protective, over-careful, over-generous...who risked smothering his child and stunting her development as a result.

She, more than most people, knew the effect a possessive, stifling love could have on a child.

She saw consternation in his eyes when they found Bambi still sleeping soundly. Too soundly? he was obviously wondering. After a brief check on Bambi's vital signs she was quick to reassure him.

'You go off duty at eleven, you said?' he asked her in an undertone, drawing her aside. The touch of his fingers on her arm almost made her noticeably recoil, not in anger or repulsion, but from shock. Did he have this potent effect on all women? she wondered dazedly, fighting for her normal composure.

'Yes, I do,' she gulped. 'But don't worry. The night nurses will keep a close check on Bambi. All through the night.'

He was frowning as he looked down at her. 'I'll be back first thing in the morning,' he said. 'But at nine-thirty I'll have to slip out for an hour or so. I have an appointment that I can't put off.'

She steeled herself to ignore the hand on her arm. 'Bambi will be fine, Mr Brody. Sister Mary Browne is in charge in the mornings. She's been here for years.' Noting the deep lines of strain in his face, she added reassuringly, 'I'll leave instructions for her or someone else to stay with Bambi while you're at your meeting. She won't be left alone.'

He pursed his lips, looking unconvinced, as if he was thinking, Nurses are busy people. They can be called away. 'Just because Bambi is quiet, and doesn't cry or scream,' he muttered, 'doesn't mean she's not feeling scared inside.'

His concern for his daughter brought a lump to her throat. 'I understand that,' she said, wishing he would let go of her arm so that she could think more clearly. 'Look,' she said on an impulse. 'I'll come myself and sit with her while you're gone.'

The grey-flecked eyes flared, before focusing on hers. 'But you don't come on duty until the afternoon. I can't expect you to do that. Aren't you catching up on your sleep in the mornings?'

She summoned a smile, feeling rather weak under his intense gaze. 'By eight in the morning I'll have had at least eight hours' sleep...'

He shook his head. 'I'll try to get my housekeeper to come in and sit with her for an hour or so. I should have thought of her before.' At Sarah's quick look he explained, 'She doesn't have much patience with children. She's over sixty and has never had children of her own. She gets nervy around kids and easily irritated.' His lip twitched faintly, but without real humour. 'She's like my mother—OK with Bambi in short doses, but that's it. However, a short stay here at the hospital shouldn't——'

'Please,' Sarah broke in. 'Don't worry, Mr Kane, if your housekeeper can't come in, or if you'd prefer not to ask her. I'll come in anyway. It will be a pleasure to come and sit with Bambi. As a visitor, not as a nurse.'

'Are you sure, Sarah?' Silver flecks glinted in his eyes as they settled on hers. It was the first time he'd used her given name and she felt a faint jolt, hearing it fall, almost like a caress, from his lips. Of course, he wasn't thinking of *her*, but of his child.

'I'm sure,' she said firmly. With a quick, nervous smile she stepped hastily back, so that he had to release his grip and let his hand slide from her arm. It was a relief to feel free of his touch... almost as if she was freeing herself of his power over her.

'Good night, Mr Kane,' she said quickly, and swinging on her heel she strode off to the nurses' station without looking back.

# CHAPTER THREE

'GOOD MORNING.' Sarah smiled as she strolled into the children's ward at nine the next morning, clasping a bulging plastic bag. Kane Brody, in a grey suit superbly tailored to his wide shoulders and lean hips, was sitting at Bambi's bedside. His daughter sat propped up on pillows, nursing a doll in her arms, her favourite frayed blanket wrapped around it.

'Sarah!' Kane rose to his feet, his eyes—more green than grey on this brighter than usual August morning—flaring faintly, as if in surprise. Because she had come? Or at the sight of her out of uniform? No doubt he disapproved of her casual sweater and thigh-hugging jeans, and the fact that she was wearing her hair loose today, in riotous disarray, instead of in the severe swept-back style she favoured for work.

His thoughts, if she had only known, were more approving than critical. He was thinking how the tumbling chestnut waves softened her rather angular features, how her bright red lipstick and red sweater gave her face vivid new life. He hadn't thought of her as beautiful, but she was, he realised.

Sarah met his gaze as it focused on hers. There was an expression in his eyes that sent a flare of heat along her cheekbones. Hadn't he expected her to come?

'How is Bambi?' she asked, flicking her gaze hastily away from the father to the child sitting up in bed. The little girl looked up at her, a glimmer of recognition—almost a smile—in her big brown eyes.

Her father answered for her. 'She seems to have no after-effects,' he said grudgingly, 'though she's still sleeping a lot. Sister Browne has just been in to check

34

her over and insists that she is fine. And Dr Graham will be in later today to decide if she can go home.'

Sarah bent over the child. 'As you see, Bambi,' she said, smiling, 'I'm here to visit you as a friend this morning, not as a nurse.' She pointed to her red woollen sweater, which had a row of fluffy white sheep across the front. 'I don't turn into a nurse again until this afternoon,' she said, explaining in a way that a three-year-old would understand. 'And by then you might have gone home...and I couldn't let you go home without saying goodbye, could I?'

Goodbye... Why did she feel a faint twinge at the thought? Was it the thought of never seeing Bambi again or...seeing the last of Kane Brody? She shook herself, mentally scoffing at the idea that it might be the latter.

She saw Bambi's gaze drift to the plastic bag in her hand, and with a smile she reached in and pulled out a yellow woollen animal. It had floppy legs, a round face, a black nose and turned-over ears.

'Oogly has come in to visit you too,' she said, sitting the stuffed animal on the edge of the bed facing Bambi.

'Oogly?' Kane Brody echoed, his whimsical drawl bringing Sarah's eyes round to meet his.

'That's what I've called him—Oogly,' she said solemnly. 'It's because he...oogles.' She shook the toy animal gently and its head lolled over. 'You see? He oogles. He sort of...flops.' The faint glitter in Kane Brody's eyes was disconcerting her. Was it amusement...or disdain? At the same time she noted that the hard planes and strained lines that had been so marked yesterday had eased, making him look rather more approachable this morning.

She turned back to Bambi, telling her gently, 'I knitted Oogly myself. I was going to give it to one of our other patients here, but...' she hesitated. 'She was too sick to look after him. So I've been keeping him at home with me, waiting for another special little girl for Oogly to visit. Only special little girls can look after ooglies. They need lots of cuddles.'

She raised the floppy animal and gave it a hug. 'Do you want to give him a cuddle?' she asked Bambi, conscious all the time she was talking that Kane Brody was watching, listening intently. She wished she knew what he was thinking.

To her delight, the child put down her doll and held out her small arms. Sarah gave her the woolly animal and watched as the child pressed it into her shoulder, wrapping her dimpled arms round it.

'I think he likes you,' Sarah said. 'If you like him too, Bambi, I think he would like to stay here with you.'

'I do like him.' The response, soft but clear, sent an odd little pang through Sarah.

She smiled gently. 'Then I think he'd like to stay with you... and even go home with you, if you would like to take him. I think he'd like to be your very own Oogly.'

The child looked up at her father with big, appealing eyes. Eyes that begged, 'Can I, Daddy?' even though she didn't ask aloud.

'If Sarah says Oogly is yours, honey, and you promise to look after him and give him lots of... cuddles——' his lips quirked and, seeing it, Sarah still couldn't be sure if it was humour he felt or mild scorn '—then of course you may. I think you should say thank you to Sarah.'

The child's big eyes swung back to Sarah's. 'Thank you,' she whispered.

'I know Oogly will be very happy with you,' Sarah said, and without looking directly at Kane Brody, she said, 'If you want to go to your meeting now, Mr Brody, Bambi and I will be fine. I'll stay here with her until you come back.'

'Sarah, thank you.' He came round the bed and stood over her, and as she looked up at him, at the power in the breadth of his shoulders, the hint of animal strength under the immaculate suit, the compelling grey-green eyes, she was aware of those same forceful vibes she had felt before, that same feeling of being almost knocked off her feet. She found she had physically to steel herself against the power of him. It was crazy!

'I really appreciate it,' he said, pinning her with his gaze. 'Especially as my housekeeper was unable to come in this morning, due to a dental appointment. But she's coming in at lunchtime to give me the chance to slip out and have some lunch. Sarah, have lunch with me.' It wasn't so much an invitation as a command. She tried not to react, to show the surprise she felt—or her resentment at his high-handed tone.

'I don't——'

'Not here at the hospital,' he cut in, a sardonic curl on his lips, as if he hadn't thought much of his canteen meal. Normally, she had no doubt, he would avoid such places like the plague. 'We'll go somewhere a little more salubrious. There's a place down by the harbour I think you might like. Everything on their menu is superb.'

I suppose he thinks I've never eaten at a decent restaurant before, Sarah thought, the hairs at the back of her neck prickling at his patronising air—or was it for some other reason? 'Thank you, but no,' she said, her tone coolly polite.

'Don't refuse me.' He dropped the arrogant tone. Now it was a softly persuasive drawl. 'Give me the chance to thank you...'

'You have thanked me,' she said, rather more sharply than she'd intended. He wasn't asking her because he wanted her company. It was simply a pay-off. Because he felt in her debt. 'Besides, I can hardly go out to lunch dressed like this!' She cast a disparaging glance down at her sweater and jeans.

He brushed that aside. 'You'll have plenty of time to go home and change before lunch. I should be back here by eleven. Earlier, if I can hasten my meeting. And then you can slip off home to change. Hilda will be here to take over from me at twelve.'

Sarah vacillated. Damn it, why not accept a free lunch? It wasn't every day a girl got wined and dined by a wealthy high-flier. So long as she kept her feet firmly on the ground and didn't go reading anything into it.

She nearly scoffed aloud at the thought. Millionaire merchant bankers didn't chase after lowly nurses like Sarah Vane. They *used* people like her. And then paid them off with a grand gesture like a lunch, wiping the slate clean.

If she had any sense, she'd keep right away from him. Already she was reacting to him in a dangerously volatile way. Dangerous to *her*. What if he did have something more than lunch in mind? A mild dalliance would mean nothing to a man like him. But what might it end up doing to *her*? She was already far too aware of him. What if she stupidly fell head over heels in love with him? Falling in love was something that must never happen—not to her. Not unless she was prepared to face the painful parting of the ways and the heartbreak that would be inevitable. Tragically, love, marriage, children must play no part in Sarah Vane's future.

'I...don't think so,' she decided finally. Let him know she wasn't bowing to his arrogant demands. *Whatever* lay behind them.

She stepped back to let him say goodbye to Bambi and explain to the child where he was going and that 'Nurse Sarah' would be staying with her until he came back. And then he was gone, the air in the ward still crackling with his presence for some time afterwards. He hadn't asked her again.

Shortly afterwards she looked up to see one of the hospital's senior administrators, Dr Fay White, marching into the ward.

'Sarah...may I speak to you for a moment?'

'Sure.' Sarah stepped away from the bed.

'Sarah, I was speaking to Mr Brody a few minutes ago. He mentioned that he had invited you out to lunch, as a thank-you for the special care you have given his daughter.'

As Sarah opened her mouth to speak, Dr White held up a hand. 'Mr Brody seemed a bit put out that you had refused him, Sarah. He thought it might have been hospital policy. I assured him it wasn't. Sarah, if he asks you again, you must accept.'

'Accept! *Why*?' Sarah faced her, half puzzled, half angry.

'We don't want to get on the wrong side of Mr Brody, Sarah. He has offered a most generous donation to the hospital. Just because he is the father of one of your patients is no reason——'

'I don't need Mr Brody's thanks,' Sarah cut in. 'It's my job to care for the children.'

'I know it is, Sarah, and you do it beautifully. But we *need* donations like Mr Brody's, and we don't want to put his back up. You mustn't refuse him again, should he ask.'

She sighed. 'Very well.' He probably wouldn't ask her again, so she was pretty safe. Men like Kane Brody didn't beg!

'Good. Well, I mustn't keep you, Sarah. It was marvellous of you to come in specially this morning to look after Bambi for Mr Brody. Let the man do something for you in return,' she said as she swept out.

Sarah glared after her.

She was reading aloud to Bambi when Kane Brody stepped into the ward. So intent were they both on the story that neither realised he was there until Sarah closed the book and heard him speak.

'You tell a story well, Sarah.' He moved closer to the bed. 'In a way a child can understand.'

She flushed as she looked up at him, aware, despite herself, of a glow of warmth at his praise. Although he wasn't openly smiling—she'd never seen him give a real smile yet, she realised—it was the closest he'd yet come to it, his well-shaped lips curving at the corners in a way she found joltingly attractive.

'I'll leave you with Bambi,' she said, stepping away from the bed. 'Goodbye, Bambi.' Her eyes softened as she looked down at the child. 'If you are still here this afternoon, I'll see you when I come on duty. I'll be a nurse again then,' she explained with a smile, swallowing as she glanced up at the child's father. Would he ask again about lunch... or not? Irrationally, she found herself waiting. Hoping?

'I'll pick you up as soon as I can after twelve,' Kane rapped at her. 'What's your address?'

She drew in her breath, her heart giving a jump. 'I——' She snapped her mouth shut again, anger overriding that initial excited flurry. The supercilious so-and-so! He wasn't even going to be gracious enough to *ask* her again! In his high-handed way, having cleverly checked first that there were no hospital rules against it, he just assumed she would meekly fall in with his plans. And there wasn't a damned thing she could do about it!

She released her breath in a sigh, capitulating as she had been ordered to do.

'My flat's only a couple of streets from the hospital,' she demurred with a shake of her head. 'Can't I——?'

'I'll still pick you up,' he insisted, and she shrugged, her lashes sweeping over her eyes to hide a glint of cynicism. Of course... He wouldn't want her coming into the hospital all dolled up for an obvious lunch-date and risk being seen escorting her out to his car. Even if Dr Fay White and the other bigwigs knew about the lunch, and approved, he wouldn't want to start tongues wagging among the nurses and staff. That would be carrying his charitable gesture too far!

'Number nine, Wells Street,' she said, her tone coolly impassive. 'I'm in flat three, but don't bother to drive in. I'll be out the front.'

'See you, then.' Still no real smile, just a twitch of his lips and a hand raised in a brief salute. She gave an answering salute, and left.

At five past twelve the sleek lines of a dark green Jaguar sedan swung into her street. A quick glimpse revealed Kane Brody at the wheel. She had been half expecting to see the silver-grey Mercedes that Beth had been driving the day before. Just how many luxury cars did this man possess?

Of course, when a man's a hot-shot merchant banker, she reminded herself with a sardonic smile as the car pulled smoothly into the kerb, he's expected to exude success, affluence and confidence.

Rather than leaping out and rushing gallantly round to open the passenger door for her, Kane flung it open from inside, rapping out, 'Jump in! I'm blocking the driveway.'

As she climbed in she cursed the fact that she was wearing a pencil-slim skirt which revealed far too much shapely leg as she settled into the soft leather bucket seat. On the other hand, she was thankful that she'd worn her chic Chanel jacket and not the pure-wool sweater she'd almost worn in its place. Sweaters, no matter how elegant and attractive, were simply not the right image for a car like this!

'You own a fleet of luxury cars?' she couldn't resist asking, a teasing smile on her lips.

The glance he tossed sideways was faintly mocking. 'Hardly a fleet,' he said drily. As he pumped the accelerator the car leapt smoothly forward like the animal after which it was named, 'I have the Jag for work and the Merc for family use, and a vintage MG sports car that I'm restoring in my spare time—vintage cars being a weakness of mine,' he confessed, a wry smile tipping the corners of his mouth. Kane Brody wouldn't have too many weaknesses, Sarah imagined.

'Then you do have some spare time?' she heard herself asking, relieved for Bambi's sake. The demands of his high-powered corporate advisory business wouldn't allow him much time off, she imagined. Why, she wondered with a slight frown, was he spending his precious spare hours restoring an old car? Why didn't he spend his spare time—every minute of it—with Bambi?

'Now and then. Tinkering with cars—using my hands, not my head for a change—helps me unwind,' Kane drawled, neatly guiding the Jag past a slow-moving truck.

At the mention of his hands, Sarah found herself idly examining the hands gripping the wheel. Strong, well-shaped hands, long-fingered and attractively brushed with fine dark hairs. Beautiful hands, she realised, flicking her tongue over her lips. Steady, capable hands, that would keep a child—or a woman—safe.

She felt heat rising to her cheeks at the thought, and with a gulp turned her thoughts instead to his daughter. 'Bambi doesn't mind you spending your evenings working out in the garage?' she asked, trying without much success to keep the censure from her voice.

She saw his dark eyebrows shoot upward. 'Did I say I spend all my evenings out in the garage?' he bit back with a tartness that drew another, even deeper, flush to her cheeks. 'On the rare occasions that I do, Bambi, I can assure you, is already in bed asleep. Working on the car is only a spare-time hobby, and spare time is something I don't have much of!'

She could have kicked herself. What right had she to question him and take him to task? She noted in dismay that the harsh, cynical lines were back in his face. And she had put them there.

'It must be tough for you bringing up a three-year-old daughter alone,' she said contritely, thinking with a rush of sympathy of the problems he must face. The constant search for a reliable nanny; the need to keep Bambi safe from harm—a need that, according to Beth, had become almost an obsession with him; the constant striving to bring happiness and security back into his small daughter's life.

*Was* the child happy? she wondered, chewing on her lip in doubt as she pictured Bambi's big pensive brown eyes. Eyes that always seemed to be waiting, searching for something...

The poor thing needed a mother, she thought with a sigh. And brothers and sisters. A warm, secure family life. Not a series of fly-by-night nannies.

'I manage. And will go on managing.' Kane Brody swung the car rather too sharply round a corner, and only Sarah's safety-belt prevented her from landing in his lap. As it was, she found her shoulder rammed up against his, her smooth cheek coming into contact with the soft cloth of his suit. The intimate contact, coming so suddenly, so unexpectedly, brought a muffled gasp to her lips and a prickling heat to her limbs.

'Sorry!' She jerked herself upright, not daring to glance up into his face, dismayed that he might have sensed her reaction, heard the faint gasp, even—heaven forbid—noticed the way she was blushing furiously—like a school-kid. How it would amuse him! Either amuse him or fill him with lofty disdain. She cursed inwardly. How galling if he had noticed! Especially as she had no designs on him whatsoever!

She set her gaze rigidly ahead, taking an abrupt interest in the lunch-hour rush, the city buildings, the great span of the Sydney Harbour Bridge ahead. She had barely noticed until now that they were heading for Circular Quay West—for the area known as The Rocks. He could be taking her to any one of a number of harbourside restaurants. Doyle's popular fish restaurant perhaps, where she had been many times before. It was always good, always well-patronised. But Kane had spoken as if the place he had chosen was...special.

'Ever been to Bilson's?' Kane asked as, miraculously, he found a parking-space by the overseas passenger terminal, only a few steps from the towering harbourside restaurant. She had seen it before, of course. It loomed over Doyle's and Circular Quay like a modern ship, all glass windows and steel railings.

'No, I haven't,' she said coolly—far more coolly than she felt. On her salary, classy restaurants like Bilson's were out. David, still studying to be a pharmacist at the time she'd been going out with him, could never have afforded to take her there, and the guys she'd dated since—usually struggling interns or junior residents working at the hospital—were more likely to take her to Doyle's or for a Chinese meal than to a place like Bilson's.

She'd always wondered what the view from Bilson's was like, knowing it claimed to have one of the finest views over the harbour. When Kane escorted her inside, where they were led across the carpeted floor to an elegant white-draped table next to the long expanse of glass that ran the full length of the restaurant, she glanced up at him, the edge of her mouth quivering.

Their view over Sydney Cove and the Opera House was blocked by a huge white cruise-ship.

Kane swore softly. He turned abruptly to the maître-d'. 'The lady would like a table with a view,' he said imperiously. 'Do you have a table upstairs?'

Sarah's hackles rose. 'The lady would like...' How did *he* know what this lady would like?

'I'm perfectly happy with this table,' she said resolutely, sliding into the chair in front of her and putting her handbag down beside her. And this is where I intend to stay, her eyes told Kane.

The eyes that met hers flared faintly. In surprise? Kane would be used to women meekly following his lead, no doubt. Or maybe he was used to women kicking up a fuss and demanding the best. The best table, the best view.

'You're happy to sit *here*?' He made no move to sit down himself, as if he was expecting her to change her mind.

'Perfectly happy.' She felt a stab of pure, fiendish pleasure. His nose, no doubt, was out of joint because now he couldn't impress her with the view!

'I'm afraid there's a private party upstairs, Mr Brody.' The maître-d' fingered his collar, as if he needed air.

'This is fine,' Sarah said firmly. 'Please sit down, Mr Brody.' I'm not one of your sophisticated, hard-to-please women-friends, her eyes reminded him. You don't have to bend over backwards to please *me*.

Kane shrugged, and glanced over his shoulder. 'Well, at least you can glimpse a bit of the harbour from where you're sitting.' He pulled out the chair opposite her and sat down at last. 'I guess we can always wave to the ship's passengers,' he said with dry humour.

She smiled, hiding her relief. He even showed signs of having a sense of humour. 'The ship looks pretty deserted to me,' she said lightly, flicking a glance over the ship's white-railed decks. 'I suppose all the passengers have gone ashore. No, not all... There's one!'

'A crew member, no doubt.' Kane's lip quirked. 'I'm sorry about this. I had no idea a ship was in.'

'Look, it doesn't matter a bit. I've seen the harbour and the Opera House plenty of times, but I've never sat overlooking the decks of a cruise-ship before.'

His eyes flickered, but he made no comment. 'You'll have wine?' he asked as a wine waiter hovered. At her nod, he ordered a bottle of Petaluma Chardonnay without consulting either her or the wine list. Fresh bread rolls appeared, and a huge menu. Their waiter recited the specials of the day, before drifting away to let them make their choice.

'How about the Atlantic salmon?' Kane suggested. 'It comes with green noodles and toasted nori. You could have the barbecued quail as a starter... or the blue swimmer crab.' He sat back, as if expecting her to bow to his expert choice. Her menu showed no prices, but she was sure he'd picked out the most expensive dishes. To impress her? she wondered, a cynical glint in her eye.

He lifted an eyebrow as she chose the fish of the day and a salad, eyeing her speculatively as she gave the waiter her order.

'No starter?' The flicker of surprise in his eyes was followed by a frown. 'Don't tell me you're one of these women who are perpetually on a diet?' He flicked a derisive glance over her slender frame.

'I'm not on a diet, no. But I'd rather have a dessert,' she confessed.

'Ah. A sweet tooth.' His mouth quirked—rather patronisingly, she thought. 'Why not have both?'

'A starter, a main course *and* a dessert?' She laughed. 'No... really, I've already had a bread roll, and if I have too much I'll fall asleep at work this afternoon.' That should hit home, she thought, wondering anew why he was going to such pains to wine and dine her in style. What she had done for his daughter hardly warranted all this attention and indulgence! And, with Bambi leaving hospital today, he must know he was unlikely ever to see her again after today.

He surprised her by ordering the same, and she flicked her tongue over her lips, unsure whether to feel flattered or patronised anew.

Over their exquisitely presented meal she summoned the courage to ask, 'Did you get in touch with Beth?'

His gaze speared hers, sharp and hard, as if demanding, Why should I be answerable to you? She steeled herself not to drop her gaze under the force of his, calmly waiting, silently willing him to answer. Which, after a tense pause, he did.

'I did.' The admission was tart. 'She declined my offer to come in and pay Bambi a last visit.' His lip curled. 'No doubt petrified she'll run into *me*. She's a gutless little thing. No backbone. No spirit.'

Sarah could imagine the imperious way he would have issued the invitation. Poor Beth!

'You mean you'd prefer a nanny who would stand up to you?' she challenged, a bantering light in her eye.

'As you do?' he drawled. For a second their eyes meshed, wrestled. She flicked her gaze away first, allowing a tiny smile to quiver on her lips to avoid a direct answer.

When he finally spoke there was a thread of respect in his voice. 'I have no argument, to this point, with the way you stand up to me, Sarah. I know you speak up from the highest of motives. You're not thinking of yourself. You're thinking of Beth, of Bambi...even of me. Of our best interests. You're obviously a caring person, Sarah.' He reached across the table and unexpectedly covered her hand with his. 'You're a fine nurse, Sarah, efficient and competent.' The ghost of a smile touched his lips, making her wonder with a faint jolt what a real smile would be like. 'And you're prepared to stand up for what you believe in.'

The warmth of his hand on hers was having a highly distracting effect on her, paralysing her muscles, even the muscles of her throat, so that she couldn't even speak.

'And you're a very attractive woman.' He lowered his voice, his gaze sliding round. 'Those businessmen at that table over there obviously agree with me. They haven't taken their eyes off you since you walked in.'

She snapped back to life, snatching away her hand, forcing her voice to unlock, furious with herself for listening to him. It was all hot air. His tone didn't even ring true. They were just words to him. Words he'd used, no doubt, thousands of times before. To numerous gullible females.

'They're more likely just curious,' she said caustically. Curious to know who Kane Brody's latest luncheon companion was. She pursed her lips. Did he think she *expected* these flowery compliments from him—on top of the food and the wine? Was this his usual way of saying thank you to a woman? Not, she must remember, that he saw her as a woman so much as his child's nurse. She was useful to him, for the time being at any rate. His daughter's well-being was in her hands, and so she must be indulged, flattered, for as long as he considered it necessary.

The man was patronising her again! Giving her what he imagined she would eagerly lap up. The great merchant banker, deigning to take his child's nurse out to lunch. Only, merely wining and dining her wasn't enough. He believed he had to spout meaningless platitudes as well, believing she was the type of woman who would expect them—and relish every syrupy utterance. Hoping to make her day, no doubt!

'Sarah... I've embarrassed you.' He'd seen his mistake, sensed her irritation, perhaps even read the thoughts racing through her mind.

'I'm not embarrassed.' Her tone was cool, rather sharp. Did he believe she'd had so few personal compliments in her life that his flattery could send her into a blushing tizzy?

'Unimpressed, then,' he said perceptively, his tone contrite now. 'I should have known you're not the type of woman who needs her vanity fed. You'd be surprised at the women who do. Who both need it and lap it up,' he said, injecting a droll, conspiratorial note. To win her round? she wondered, still not trusting him.

'Forgive me?' he pressed, tilting his head at her, the green-flecked eyes a magnetic lure.

She resisted them, though she did smile—if a trifle unsteadily. 'Begging doesn't suit you,' she told him lightly. He wouldn't be a man to beg often or easily, she had a feeling.

She caught her breath as an answering smile inched his lips apart, a smile that spread slowly, bringing intriguing new creases to the area round his eyes and breaking up the hard cynical lines of his face. The first real smile she had seen! And, as she'd imagined...it was dynamite!

To cover her startled reaction she said the first thing that popped into her head. 'You should smile more often.' Deciding to go for broke, she gritted her teeth and went a step further. 'It has a most humanising effect.'

She gulped as his smile faded, though mercifully without any harsh stiffening of his features. 'You think I need humanising?' he asked in a tone of quiet mockery.

'Well...' What could she say? There was a limit to her frankness. 'I barely know you,' she countered. 'I...only met you yesterday.' And by tomorrow—or maybe even this afternoon—he would be gone again, out of her life forever. And little Bambi too. The thought brought a pang of regret.

'Sarah Vane, I have a feeling you already know more about me than most people who've known me a lifetime.' He was looking at her with an unnerving intensity, in a way that made her lower her gaze and take a sudden interest in the pattern on her plate, already scraped clean of the blueberry *crème brulée* she'd chosen for dessert.

'Maybe it's more a gut feeling on your part at this stage,' he added in a silky drawl. 'There's something about me that you disapprove of, isn't there, Sarah?'

The seductive note in his voice raised the hairs at her nape. She had the feeling that he *was* trying to seduce her. With his voice, his eyes, his probing questions. But *why*? Was he such a rake that he couldn't help himself?

She swallowed before looking up at him. 'Of course, there isn't,' she denied, giving herself a tiny shake and trying to dredge up some good, positive things about him. There was his love for Bambi, of course, and the way he'd stayed by his daughter's side for all those long hours yesterday. And the way he was so anxious to have someone sit with her today when he couldn't be there with her himself.

She wasn't so sure about his motives for inviting his child's nurse out to lunch today. He *could* have asked her simply out of kindness, out of gratitude, just as he'd said. It was just possible that she had been maligning him by imagining he had something less noble in mind...like taking advantage of a naïve young nurse for his own wolfish gratification!

She caught the speculative glint in his eyes, and a shimmer of something else that she was unable to decipher. At the same time she had the weirdest feeling that he had been reading her own thoughts with unnerving accuracy.

'Something tells me that you're a fair person, Sarah...that you prefer to dwell on a person's good points rather than their faults.' His mouth gave a wry twist. 'Some of which, in my case, you have already witnessed. Impatience being one of them. A rotten temper another. And throwing my weight around. I hope you won't hold them against me.'

Her eyelashes fluttered, shuttering her eyes. With a whimsical smile she said, 'It's people who can't see their own faults who are beyond redemption.'

'So...' A dark eyebrow shot up. 'You don't think I am?'

'Beyond redemption?' She slanted a look at him, a flicker of cautious amusement in her eyes. 'That depends on what your other faults are. The ones you haven't admitted to.'

'You're a hard woman, Sarah.' But his tone was benign now, tolerant. He was no fool. He'd sensed her mistrust and had cooled it for now. Or lost interest. 'Coffee?' he asked, and she nodded.

When it came she assumed a clipped business-like tone to ask, 'Have you decided yet who is going to look after Bambi when she goes home?' He would hardly have had time yet to find a new nanny. And it would be difficult for him, she imagined, with the high-pressured job he had, to keep taking days off work.

'My housekeeper Hilda has a married niece, Meryl, who's offered to come in for a few hours each day, at least until I find a regular nanny.' He waved a hand for the bill as he spoke. 'With her two boys now at school,

Meryl's able to come during school hours to look after Bambi, though she'll have to leave again at three to pick them up from school.'

'What's going to happen after three?' Sarah asked as he checked and signed the bill.

'I'll make sure I'm home by then,' he said, glancing at her. The look in his eye was cool and enigmatic rather than resentful at her probing. 'It will only be for a while... until I find a new nanny for Bambi.'

Sarah drew in a careful breath before asking, 'Does Bambi get on well with Meryl?' It worried her that the child had no constant mother-figure whom she could depend on for a loving relationship on a regular basis. This procession of short-lived caretakers couldn't be good for her.

'Meryl has babysat Bambi before, on the odd evening I've had no nanny available and needed to go out.' His tone was curt now, bordering on impatient. 'Meryl's a sensible woman, used to young children. I can rely on her.' More than he could rely on Beth, he seemed to be implying. 'Ready to go?' he asked, checking his watch. He would be keen, naturally, to get back to Bambi. And keen to get away from *her* and her searching questions? Sarah wondered ruefully as she reached for her purse.

He had dropped the seductive drawl, which only reinforced her opinion that it had just been an act. Had he decided she wasn't worth the bother?

'It was a most pleasant lunch, Mr Brody,' she said with prim politeness as she stood up. 'Thank you.'

'Call me Kane, Sarah, please. At least outside the hospital,' he said in a mocking drawl as he stepped round to guide her from the restaurant.

She flicked her tongue over her lips. 'If you like.' There it was again, lurking under the mockery—that sensual, provocative curl in his voice. Was he doing it just to make her feel good? Knowing they were unlikely to meet again after today? Knowing he was safe?

She sighed. Why *was* he being so friendly and attentive? Purely because she was his child's nurse and
had been taking a special interest in Bambi?

But... did she *deserve* to be singled out? She was only
*one* of Bambi's nurses, after all.

# CHAPTER FOUR

SARAH wasn't sure what made her come on duty half an hour early. Some sixth sense, she later thought. She only knew, when she walked into the children's ward at half past two and met Kane Brody leaving with Bambi in his arms, that she felt a rush of relief. A few minutes later and she would have missed them, missed the chance to say goodbye.

'Dr Graham has been in already?' she asked stupidly, knowing full well that they wouldn't be leaving without his permission.

'Ah, Sarah!' Kane Brody's face eased into one of his rare smiles, at once disarming her, plucking an answering smile from her. 'We weren't running off without thanking you and saying goodbye.'

She eyed him uncertainly. They weren't? With Bambi and the child's toys and clothes in his arms? 'There was no need——' she began lamely, breaking off to add in a rush, 'I'm glad I have the chance to say goodbye to Bambi. I——'

'I left a note for you, Sarah,' Kane intervened smoothly, 'inviting you to our home tomorrow for lunch. I know Bambi would be delighted if you would come. You could check her over at the same time, if it wouldn't be imposing on you too much.'

She was tongue-tied for a second, as an unexpected zing of excitement bubbled through her. 'I... That would be...' Oh hell, she thought, mentally kicking herself. Why am I stammering? He's still anxious about his daughter, that's all it is, and he wants a nurse to pop in and check her over. He won't even be there himself. He's getting a babysitter in for the day, remember?

53

On top of that thought came another. This must be what he had been angling for over lunch yesterday...

'If you like, Sarah,' he said in the same smooth drawl, 'I'll pick you up on my way home from work. It'll save giving you directions.'

'You're coming home at lunchtime?'

'I don't want to be away from Bambi for too long at the moment, even with Meryl there during the day. Meryl can drive you home in the afternoon in time for your hospital shift, on her way to pick her boys up from school.'

'But it might be out of her way. Let me bring my own car...'

'No arguments.' His tone warned that one argued with Kane Brody at one's peril. 'Meryl won't mind. She's always willing to help. Always dependable. A damned sight more dependable than that so-called highly-skilled nanny I paid so much for.'

'I'm sure Beth's learned her lesson,' Sarah murmured.

'Always so tolerant...so fair-minded!' There was a mildly baffled, almost brooding note in his voice, as if he hadn't seen much fairness in his life. Perhaps, Sarah mused, in the business he was in, the tough, cut-throat world of merchant banking, fairness didn't feature high. Second chances, no doubt, would not be considered.

She shifted her gaze to Bambi, smiling as she said, 'I'll come and visit you tomorrow, Bambi. Would you like that?'

The child nodded, her soft lips trembling in the beginning of a smile. 'I'll look after Oogly,' she promised in a shy whisper.

Sarah reached out to stroke the child's small, dimpled arm—only to lower her head on an impulse and kiss the child on the cheek.

To her surprised delight the little girl curled an arm round her neck and kissed her in return, a warm, moist, fervent kiss that connected with the edge of her mouth.

As she stepped away, flushing with pleasure, Sarah felt Kane Brody's eyes on her. Glancing up, she caught the startled gleam in his eyes and was struck by his taut, strained expression.

Did he resent the spontaneous gesture? Resent the eager way his child had kissed a virtual stranger?

Or was he thinking back...? Thinking of his tragic young wife, Bambi's mother? Of the emptiness in their lives, the bitter loss they'd both suffered? An emptiness that no nurse, no nanny, no caretaker, could ever fill?

All morning Sarah half expected the phone to ring, for Kane Brody—or his secretary, perhaps, calling on his behalf—to announce that he had an unexpected business meeting or some other pressing engagement that meant he would have to cancel her visit to his home.

But no call came, and at twelve, on the dot of the hour he'd designated, his sleek Jaguar swung into her street and pulled into the kerb where she stood waiting.

She had no worry today, as she climbed into his car, about baring her knees to his gaze. Her black flared skirt fell in soft folds round her ankles as she eased herself into the soft bucket seat beside his. Since they were going to his home this time and not to a restaurant, she had dressed more informally, choosing the soft woollen sweater she'd thought of wearing the day before.

'That soft blue suits you, Sarah,' Kane commented as he drove off. 'It brings out the blue of your eyes. If you'll accept the compliment,' he muttered drily in the same breath. 'I know you don't care for personal remarks.'

'I've nothing against a genuine off-the-cuff compliment,' she said with a quick smile. 'It's only when they're—well——'

'Contrived?'

'Mmm. Or just said to——' she shrugged '—butter a girl up. When it's empty flattery. Meaningless.' Take note, Kane Brody.

He did. 'I'll keep that in mind,' he vowed, his tone coolly impersonal, leaving her uncertain if he was amused or had genuinely taken her words to heart.

She hastily switched the subject. 'How's Bambi? Happy to be home again?'

'Happy...' He considered the word. 'My daughter doesn't often show much outward sign of the way she feels. She can be a trifle...withdrawn. Shy,' he admitted. An admission, Sarah sensed, that came with reluctance. 'You, however, Sarah, seem to have a knack of drawing her out. In your company, for any period of time, I am sure she would...blossom.'

In the long pause that followed, Sarah felt her heart pick up a beat. What was he saying? Surely he couldn't mean that he wanted to see more of...? No! To Kane Brody she was simply his child's nurse, nothing more. Which was fine by her, just fine. She would never *want* to be more—never *could* be more.

He spoke again, saving her from comment. 'Do you realise, Sarah, that when Bambi kissed you yesterday...?' Again he paused, as if he was having difficulty finding the words he wanted. 'It was the first time,' he confessed with a twist of his lips, 'that she has willingly kissed anybody but me. And even I don't always get a kiss without asking for it.'

Sarah drew in a tremulous breath, at a loss to know how to answer, what to say. She sensed that the admission hadn't come easily to him, and she didn't want to spoil this rare baring of his soul by saying the wrong thing and seeing him clam up again, seeing his face harden into the cynical, coldly indomitable mask that Beth had found so intimidating. It would be a pity...just as he was starting to open up a bit.

Next moment, to her open-mouthed astonishment, he pulled into the side of the road and jerked the car to an abrupt halt. She glanced out of the side window. He couldn't live here... There were no houses anywhere in sight. Only a park and a school...

She felt his hand touch her arm, her nerve-ends jumping in startled response. 'Tell me Sarah, I have to know. It's been puzzling me since yesterday. Why are you leaving?'

'Leaving?' She turned to face him, confusion bringing a silvery-blue glitter to her eyes.

'Leaving the hospital. Giving up your job.'

Her eyes widened. 'You *know* I'm leaving? How...? Who...?' She was flustered by the searching look in his eyes, the intensity in his voice.

'Dr Graham told me. Why, was it meant to be confidential?' Curiosity flickered in his eyes. 'I understand you're planning to leave at the end of the week, so you must have handed in your notice some time ago.'

'That's right.' She swallowed. 'No, there's no secret about it.' She was just surprised that he knew, that the subject had even come up. Had Dr Graham volunteered the information, or had Kane Brody been asking questions about her? Checking her out!

He seemed to read the unspoken question in her eyes. 'I was telling Dr Graham how grateful I was for the care you've been giving Bambi, the special understanding you seem to have. I feel I haven't adequately thanked you myself.'

'But you have.' She flushed. 'Please, there's no need.'

He didn't press it. He wouldn't be a man to labour a point, she imagined. Let alone grovel!

'Dr Graham was saying what an excellent nurse you are and how sorry the hospital will be to lose you. So...' The magnetic force of his gaze caught and held hers. 'What are you intending to do, Sarah, when you leave? Nurse somewhere else? Get married? Travel overseas?'

She dragged her gaze away from his, needing to escape the feeling of being caught in his power—needing to show herself she *could* escape. 'I intend to go on nursing. The flying doctor service has been advertising for nurses. I've applied for a job with them.'

'The flying doctor service?' She heard the surprise in his voice. 'Why would you want to go and work in the outback?'

'Why not?' She shrugged. 'The outback *needs* nurses.'

'The remoteness wouldn't bother you? The loneliness, the heat?'

'I've been up north before.' She lifted her chin. 'I know what to expect.' No need to tell him she'd only been as far as Alice Springs and Ayers Rock on a bus camping-trip. 'And no, none of those things would bother me. Not a bit.'

'You don't have a...boyfriend? Plans to settle down?'

'No, I don't!' she snapped, far more sharply than he deserved. But what business was it of his?

'Well, why should you want to settle down? You're young. There's plenty of time.'

His patronising tone caught her on the raw. 'I'm twenty-six years old,' she bit back, 'and, even if I were thirty-six, it would make no difference. I have no plans to marry. Ever. I—I'm not the marrying type!'

She saw something glimmer deep in his eyes. Surprise? *Relief*? She felt a quick flare of resentment, verging on anger. Surely he couldn't have thought...?

Damn you, Kane Brody, she fumed inwardly, I suppose it comes as a great relief to you to know that I don't have any designs on you—a great relief that I didn't let your invitation today, or the one yesterday, give me the dumb idea that your interest in me was *personal*!

'When are you planning to go bush?' Kane asked, without commenting on her impassioned statement.

As she gulped down her feeling of outrage she had the feeling he was waiting intently for her answer. Why *was* he so interested in her future plans? she wondered in quick suspicion.

Taking a deep breath, she forced herself to simmer down, to see things from his side. Men in Kane Brody's position, she guessed, had reason to be wary. Being the filthy-rich, highly eligible widower that he was, *and* a real hunk at the same time—a *spunk*, as Paula had called him—he must have women chasing after him all the time.

It must be very tedious. On the other hand, maybe he enjoyed having women on tap! Unless he'd sworn off women since his wife's death.

She thought of Bambi and let out her breath in a sigh. Whatever *his* needs, surely he must want to find a new mother for his child, if not yet, at least some time in the future? Or didn't he want to share Bambi with anyone else again, ever? Maybe he felt that no other women could ever replace the wife he'd lost so abruptly and so tragically.

'Sarah?'

'Oh. Sorry.' He'd asked her a question. 'Actually,' she said, and paused, wondering how much to tell him. Not too much, she decided. 'I'm going to take a short holiday first. I haven't had one for nearly a year. I have friends up in the Blue Mountains who've been urging me to come up and stay.'

'The Blue Mountains?' He raised a sardonic eyebrow. 'Nothing more adventurous? Like a trip overseas?'

'Trips overseas cost money,' she flung back, and then wished she hadn't. What would Kane Brody know or care about money problems? About a daughter who needed to give financial assistance to a widowed mother? About a mother who insisted on clinging to the old family home, even though it was run-down and constantly in need of repair and maintenance?

'Hadn't we better get on our way?' She spoke brusquely, to evade further probing. Aren't you anxious to see how your daughter is? was what she meant. Knowing how obsessed Kane Brody was with his daughter, it surprised her that he would let anything delay him from getting to her as quickly as possible. Again she found herself pondering on why her resignation from the hospital and her plans for the future should have sparked this interest in him.

Surely... Her heart missed a beat. Surely he hadn't been thinking of asking her to become Bambi's new *nanny*? It wasn't unknown for nurses to switch to home care. Of course, now that he knew about her plans to work in the outback, he'd know there would be no point in asking. Not that she would ever have considered it anyway... getting so closely involved in a family situation. And especially not with *this* family. With this daughter... this father... this dynamo of a man.

She felt a tiny shiver feather down her spine. Personal involvement was something she had to guard carefully against. At least where there was the slightest risk that it could lead to a serious involvement of the heart. That, cruelly, sadly, *unfairly*, was something she had to avoid at all costs.

Kane's voice broke into her sober thoughts. 'You're absolutely right.' The new buoyant note in his voice surprised her, puzzling her anew, even bringing a faint pang of regret as he turned back to the wheel. 'High time we were on our way!'

She wondered at the self-satisfied smile on his lips.

From a visual point of view Kane's ultra-modern home, one of a row of impressive harbourside homes in Sydney's exclusive 'bankers' belt', was a stunner. The multi-level house jutted precariously out of the rocky cliff-face, its huge windows and broad sundecks giving kaleidoscopic views over the harbour.

But it struck Sarah that it wasn't the ideal place to bring up a small child, with its hazardous rocky cliff and the steep steps and the danger of the water below. No wonder Kane had become so protective, so obsessed with his child's safety and well-being! It must be a nightmare watching over her.

When she ventured to ask about it, Kane said curtly, 'Bambi doesn't play anywhere but in the house or on the decks. It's far too dangerous.' His voice had chilled slightly, as if he didn't relish her implied criticism. 'The sundecks provide more than adequate room for her to play. And the house has plenty of space inside.'

An understatement! The bright spaciousness of the interior hit Sarah forcibly as Kane waved her in through the impressive double doors.

Whoever had decorated his home—surely a professional decorator?—had produced a house of breathtaking beauty and style, but it belonged, Sarah thought, as her initial stunned awe subsided, in a magazine rather than to a real flesh-and-blood family with a young growing child. She wondered how anyone could comfortably relax in a house with velvet-smooth white carpet throughout, with loungers and armchairs covered in the palest ice-blue silk which must have cost a fortune and must show every mark, and with delicately balanced sculptures and fragile pieces of the finest porcelain and china in every corner, on every table. Even the television set had been discreetly banished from sight behind an exotic inlaid timber cabinet.

But she bit back any comment, remembering Kane's wife in time. The interior décor would almost certainly have been her choice—with or without professional help—and any criticism of the house would be criticism of her. Kane might have strong feelings about keeping it precisely the way she had left it. He and his wife could even have chosen the décor together, wanting a home they could show off to Kane's influential colleagues and high-flying friends.

All that mattered was how Bambi was doing, and whether she was suffering any after-effects as a result of her accident. After all, Sarah mused, that was why she had been invited here. To check on Bambi's state of health.

'I told Meryl to keep Bambi in bed until you had checked her over,' Kane told her as he led her through one stunning room after another.

'Oh, there was no need to keep her in...' Sarah trailed off under the withering look he gave her. 'I mean, as long as she's kept quiet and isn't allowed to run riot for a few days...' She spoke with a smile, trying to imagine Bambi ever being allowed to run riot. Certainly not in this house. And outside? Well, it simply wouldn't be safe.

She blinked as Kane waved her into the nursery. A palace of a room, the most spacious child's room she had ever seen, exquisitely wallpapered and furnished, with delicate mobiles dangling from the ceiling. What struck her most of all was the room's amazing neatness. Nothing appeared out of place, or the worse for wear, or even much used, come to that—let alone loved to death. The dolls and toys and books lining the shelves could have come straight from the store.

Unbidden, the term 'gilded cage' sprang to her mind.

Bambi was sitting up in her pretty Queen Anne bed, clutching Oogly in her arms. A young woman with fuzzy ginger hair broke off the story she was reading aloud and rose hastily from her chair.

'Meryl, this is Sister Sarah Vane, from the hospital,' Kane said, making sure that his babysitter was under no false illusions about his guest.

'Bambi's fine, Mr Brody,' Meryl assured him in a breathy voice before he could put the question to her.

'I see you've pulled back the curtains.' Kane frowned towards the bright light streaming in through the expanse of glass. The windows framed yet another fine view of the harbour, the water a slash of deep blue under the wintry sky.

'Bambi assured me the light didn't disturb her eyes or give her a headache,' Meryl said quickly.

Kane's brow plunged further. 'Yes, she would. Bambi never complains.' He tossed an enquiring look at Sarah. 'Shouldn't she be kept in a darkened room for a few days?'

Sarah glanced at Bambi, gave her a quick smile, and said, 'Oh, no, I don't think so. Not if the light's not bothering her. I'm sure that Meryl, having young children of her own, would know if it was.' She moved closer to the bed, and, adopting her nurse's guise, leaned over to peer deep into the child's big brown eyes.

'Well, Bambi,' she said, taking the child's wrist and feeling for her pulse, 'it's good to see you again. Did Oogly sleep well?'

The child nodded, looking up at her, mute with shyness, but managing the flicker of a smile.

'Good. And what about you, Bambi? Did you sleep well too?'

Another nod, eyes big and unblinking.

'No headaches?' Sarah brushed her fingers over the child's smooth brow. 'Has your head been hurting at all?'

'No.'

'Good. Perhaps you would like to get out of bed for a while?' Sarah suggested, and saw the child look up at her father, her eyes wide in silent appeal.

'Well, since Sarah says it's all right...' Kane gave a nod. 'Meryl, you could dress Bambi while I show Sarah the view from the sundeck. We'll have lunch in the sunroom—it's a bit too cool outside. I like to have my meals with my daughter whenever I can,' he told Sarah as they moved away from the bed. 'She might not eat as much as I'd like, but she manages quite well for a three-year-old.'

'I'm nearly four,' piped up a small voice as Bambi plucked herself from her shyness to set him straight.

'Well, that's right, so you are. In just two weeks from now.' Kane's eyes held a rare tenderness as he paused to look back at his daughter, but Sarah sensed something else in his expression as he glanced away. A darkening, a hardness. Because his wife wouldn't be there to share the birthday?

As Kane led her out he growled, 'I only wish she would eat more,' and Sarah wondered if that was behind the look she had seen. Or was he just trying to cover up his pain?

'Well, don't force her,' she said lightly. 'She'll pick up in time.' When she gets more confidence, she added to herself, and is given a chance to run around more. Where was there to run here? Only in her room and out on the decks! No wonder Beth had had to take her to the park to play.

When Meryl was ready to drive her home at the end of her visit, Kane, with Bambi in his arms, came to see them both off, Meryl having parked her car in the street outside Kane's impressive triple garage. Sarah gave Bambi a quick hug and reminded her to give Oogly lots of cuddles, making no promise to come back and see her again in case Kane gave her no chance. This time Bambi made no move to kiss her, simply nodding shyly, as if she had received too many knock-backs in her short life to expect anything much of anyone.

'Bambi, run over and say goodbye to Meryl,' Kane said, putting his daughter down. 'Sarah, thank you for coming,' he said, lowering his voice. 'Would you consider coming again tomorrow? Another of Hilda's fine lunches—in return for checking on Bambi?' The steady eyes that held hers were a compelling sage-green in the bright wintry sunlight. Sure, no doubt, of their power. Sure of her compliance. 'If it's still fine, and a bit warmer, we could have lunch out on the sundeck.'

She hesitated. Was he really thinking only of Bambi, or was there something else behind the invitation, behind the magnetic appeal in his eyes? If only she knew!

The only way to find out was to ask. 'Kane, you're not...?' She bit her lip, asking in a rush, 'You're not hoping to talk me out of joining the flying doctor service, are you? In the hope that I'll take on the job of—of your daughter's nanny instead?'

Kane stared at her, his eyes flaring in what seemed genuine surprise. Then he threw back his head in a gust of laughter, abruptly cut off. His hand shot out to clamp on her arm. 'Sarah, nothing could be further from my mind. I'm asking you because...' He paused, as if making up his mind about something. 'OK, I admit it's not just so that you can check on Bambi,' he said, his voice velvety smooth...persuasive. 'It's because she sees you as a friend, Sarah. As I do. Is it so wrong to ask you to visit...as a friend?'

She felt a deep tremor run through her, but wasn't sure if it was caused by the touch of his hand on her arm or the thought that he wanted her for a friend. Not just a friend for Bambi, but for himself as well.

Precisely what kind of friend did he have in mind? she wondered, her stomach knotting at the thought.

She realised he was waiting for an answer. And Meryl was starting to look anxious. 'N-no. I guess not,' she said at length, weakening. She was over-reacting again... He just wanted her to drop in as a friend. Nothing more. 'All right. I'd... be pleased to come again tomorrow. Thank you.'

She would be gone soon anyway...to the Blue Mountains to have a much-needed holiday, and after that to the remote outback to work indefinitely. Kane knew she was going, so he would hardly be expecting their friendship to blossom into anything more. A brief platonic friendship, that was all he had in mind. For Bambi's sake.

As he'd said, was there anything wrong with visiting as a friend?

# CHAPTER FIVE

FIFTEEN minutes before Kane was due to pick her up the next day her front doorbell rang. Hairbrush poised in mid-air, Sarah felt her heart skip a beat. Had Kane arrived early and decided to park his car at the front and come in?

Luckily she was already dressed and ready to go, but... She glanced round quickly, groaning at the chaotic state her flat was in. Too late, darn it, to do anything about it now!

She dropped her hairbrush and stood back for a last critical look in the mirror, wondering belatedly if her striped blouse and grey trousers were a bit casual for the stunning Brody mansion. With a sigh she swung round and hastened to the door.

'Kane!' At the sight of his tall, imposing frame in her doorway, tiny sparks raced along her nerves. 'Am I late? I'm sorry you had to come in and fetch me,' she heard herself babbling. 'I hope you didn't have any trouble finding a place to park?'

'No trouble at all.' He rested an indolent hand on the doorframe. 'And no, you're not late. I'm early.'

'I—I'll just fetch my purse.'

'Aren't you going to ask me in?' He spoke in a lazy drawl, seeming in no hurry to go.

Had he come early deliberately? She gave him a quick, sharp look. The light was behind him, making it difficult to read his expression, the shadowed eyes. What did he want? To give her flat the once-over, to see if her living conditions came up to the standard required of a friend of the Brody family?

'Sorry.' She stepped back, eyeing him warily. 'Please...come in.' Maybe he'd come for some other

66

reason. To call off her visit to his home, perhaps. She felt a swift dip in her spirits at the thought. She had been looking forward to seeing Bambi again. Only Bambi? a niggling voice teased.

'Nice flat,' Kane commented as he stepped inside.

She tossed him a disbelieving look, thinking of his own spectacular, immaculate home. 'I'm afraid it's in a bit of a mess.' What must he think of all the books and magazines cluttering the shelves and coffee-table, the motley assortment of artefacts she'd collected over the years, the lumpy, over-sized cushions on the floor, the records and tapes strewn around the stereo-player? The room seemed to shrink as his gaze swept round. Her entire flat would just about fit into one of his own bathrooms!

'It's charming. Warm and homely and...inviting.'

'You mean it has its own *quaint* charm,' she said with a wry smile. What was he up to? He was laying it on with a trowel! 'Would you like to sit down?'

'Thanks.' He chose one of her two old armchairs—rejects from her mother's house. As he lowered himself down his body sank deep into its comfortable softness, his long legs sprawled out in front of him.

She giggled. She couldn't help it. 'You may have trouble getting up again,' she warned.

'I may not want to. It's sinfully comfortable.'

Even that word 'sinfully' seemed deliberate. It was as if he was carefully setting some scene of his own. But for what? 'It's a very old armchair. It came from my old home,' she managed to respond. She chose one of the upright chairs for herself, perching on its edge as she wondered tensely what was coming.

'How long since you left home?' he asked easily, leaning back into the soft cushions.

Had he just dropped in for a *chat*? Because he was running a few minutes early?

'I moved out when I started my nurse training,' she told him. 'My mother still lives in our old home. It's really too big for her, and the garden too, but I can't persuade her to move.'

'She lives alone?'

'Yes.' She felt a warmth in her cheeks, and was annoyed that she wasn't yet over the guilt of leaving her mother. 'My father died a few years ago. After I'd left home.'

'Any brothers or sisters?'

'Unfortunately, no. My mother wasn't able to have any more children after I was born. She always said she was lucky she had *me*. Before I came along she'd had a number of miscarriages.' Was *this* the reason Kane had dropped in? To quiz her about her family, her background? To find out more about her? To see if she was a fit and acceptable person to go on visiting his daughter?

'Did Bambi have a good night?' She tossed the question at him before he could probe any further into her family history. 'She's with Meryl again this morning?' She was puzzled that Kane wasn't in more of a hurry to get home to her.

'Slept like a baby. She's showing no sign of headaches or any other after-effects.'

'She's bounced back very well,' Sarah agreed. 'Children are tougher than you think.' It wouldn't hurt, she decided, to remind him of that. To point out that it wasn't necessary to treat his child like a fragile piece of glass.

'She's looking forward to your visit today, Sarah. She's really taken to you. To you *and* Oogly.' His mouth twitched. 'Thanks to Oogly, she's lost interest in that rotten old blanket of hers. So you've done me a favour, Sarah. Another one, I should say.'

Her eyes met his, and something in the way he was watching her, his gaze speculative under his half closed lids, started a nervous skittering in her chest. For want of something—anything—to say to fill the pause that followed, she blurted out, 'You have a beautiful home,

Kane.' Practical or not, it was certainly that. A visual delight.

'Beautiful?' He looked faintly startled. As if he didn't think of it in that light. As if, to him, it was just...home.

His reaction disarmed her. While his house might not be her cup of tea—as a home to feel comfortably relaxed in—visually it was spectacular, the brilliance of the harbour seeming to flow into every room. Kane probably found it very peaceful. 'It's the most stunningly beautiful house I've ever seen,' she said truthfully.

He shrugged, his mouth twisting. 'So it damn well ought to be. It cost enough to get it the way my——' He clamped his mouth shut, plainly annoyed with himself for lowering his guard.

'The way your wife wanted it?' Sarah finished quietly. Talk about her, Kane, she silently appealed to him. Don't keep bottling up your feelings, your anger, your anguish, your resentment, or whatever it is that you feel.

His brow darkened ominously at the mention of his wife. For a second she thought he was rejecting her plea, closing her out. Then he spoke, his lips barely parting as he muttered tightly, 'I gave her a free hand with the house. It was worth it...at the time.'

A whole range of turbulent emotions blazed in his eyes as he uttered the taut words. Pain, regret, bitterness, frustration... She would have sworn she saw them all. Pain because his wife had had so little time to enjoy the home she'd created? Regret that she had been snatched so prematurely from his life? Bitterness at the cruel unfairness of life? Frustration that he had been unable to prevent what had happened to her?

'It's a beautiful house, Kane,' she repeated. It must be hard, painfully hard for him, she thought, not being able to share all that stunning beauty with the woman who had created it, the woman he had loved so intensely that he could hardly bear to talk about her, even now, nearly two years later. 'And such fantastic views over the harbour,' she enthused. 'Glorious. At night it must be truly magical.' Whatever she thought of the house as a home to live in—or as a suitable place to bring up a child—the views she could rave about wholeheartedly.

'You think so, do you?' Kane's voice was flat now, all emotion drained away, or brutally wiped out. With a grunt he gripped the arms of his chair and hauled himself to his feet.

As she was about to rise too she found herself flopping back with a tiny gasp. Kane stood over her, restraining her with an inflexible hand on her shoulder. His face hovered above hers, his piercing gaze trapping her own. 'You think it's beautiful, *but*——?'

She swallowed. 'But?' she echoed, dismayed that he had seen through her after all.

'I sense a "but" in there somewhere.'

Her eyes wavered under the force of his gaze. 'No, truly, Kane, I...'

'You're a tactful person, Sarah, but your eyes are more expressive than you think. What is it that you disapprove of?'

'Disapprove? Kane, what in the world makes you think I——?'

'Tell me, Sarah!' Catching her slender wrists in his hands, he tugged her to her feet and pulled her close, far too close for comfort, with only her bent forearms between them, pressed up against his chest. His eyes still held hers captive, the grey flecks in the green burning silver-bright under her gaze, mesmerising her. She felt a choking sensation, as if her breath was being sucked from her lungs.

'*But*?' His voice rumbled through her body, deep, vibrant, insistent.

She stared helplessly up at him. How could she even think straight, let alone talk and make sense, with him holding her so close, looking at her the way he was, his paralysing gaze threatening to devour her, swallow her whole?

'*But*?' he repeated, and she heard the steel in his voice.

She sighed. He was giving her no choice! Somehow she managed to find her voice, but the words came haltingly, with difficulty. 'Well... To me, Kane—stunning as it is—it's more a—a house to admire than a—a real rough-and-tumble home to, well, to bring up young children in.' She faltered under the flickering flame in his eyes.

'I don't want a rough-and-tumble home.' His tone was wintry now, distant. 'I have a young daughter, not a houseful of larrikin sons.'

She trembled under the iron grip of his hands on her wrists. 'No... of course. But, Kane, won't Bambi ever want to have friends over to play? From kindergarten? Or later from school? You *are* planning to send her to kindergarten?'

'Next year. Perhaps.' He shrugged the problem aside. 'Bambi's room and the sundecks are big enough for a whole tribe of kids.'

'You'd bar them from the rest of the house?' she ventured, a determined recklessness driving her on.

'Of course not,' he said irritably. 'It's a home, not a sh——' She would have sworn he was about to say 'shrine', but what he finally came out with was 'glasshouse'.

'You won't mind them scuffling around on your white carpet and putting their grubby fingers all over those delicate chairs and cushions and knocking your precious Lladro and Lalique pieces flying?' She managed an arch look, wishing he would let her go.

'I'd see that they didn't *have* grubby fingers or wear shoes inside. And breakables can easily be removed,' was his growling response.

Obviously, he didn't see it as a problem. 'Well, as long as you're——'

'What else?' he rapped, his grip tightening. The air between them held almost a physical turbulence, sending a quivering shudder through her. 'You've gone this far. Don't hold back now!'

Valiantly, she tilted her chin. 'All right. It's not . . . all that safe, is it? You think a growing child will never want to clamber over those tempting rocks? Never try to get down to the water?'

His eyes narrowed. He seemed to repress a shudder. 'Why do you think I watch over my daughter like a hawk? And employ nannies at exorbitant expense? To protect her from those dangers! Damn it, Sarah, I'm raising her to be a lady, not a tomboy!'

'Kane, you can't keep her confined all the time. It's like keeping a bird in a cage.' She tried to ignore the fingers biting into her flesh. 'You'll only end up repressing her, taking away her initiative, her courage. She'll come to rely on you for everything. She'll end up never being able to do a thing for herself!'

She took a gasping breath, staring up at Kane in dismay. Oh, hell, now she *had* gone too far!

'Kane, forgive me!' she cried before he had a chance to speak. 'I——'

'Forget it,' he rasped, still not releasing his grip on her. 'I did ask.' His face was coldly impassive now; like a rock, his eyes shuttered, giving her no clue to what he was thinking, whether he was angry—angry with her for speaking out against him, or with himself for asking in the first place—or whether, just possibly, she had given him food for thought. She doubted it! The Kane Brodys of this world seldom doubted themselves, let alone admitted they could be wrong. When they made a decision it would be as fixed, as inflexible as setting it in concrete.

'L-let me get my purse,' she mumbled, but instead of letting her go he hauled her, with a breath-stopping jerk, hard up against the wall of his chest.

'That took courage, Sarah, standing up to me like that.' He gave a low growl in his throat. 'Mmm, you smell good. . .' He slid his arms round her. 'You *feel* good.'

Dazed, she stared up at him, her tongue flicking nervously over her lips. She saw his gaze slide to her mouth...felt a wave of heat flow up her throat to flood her cheeks. In that instant she knew instinctively what was coming. She found herself paralysed, waiting, *wanting* it to happen. And then his face blurred as his mouth smothered hers.

The hungry pressure of his lips, moist and sensual on the warm softness of hers, came as a shock that sent deep trembling waves rolling through her body. Her response was instinctive, her lips parting, quivering under his, her bones tingling, dissolving, her pliant body melting into the rippling contours of his.

He pulled back as if scalded—or shocked, more likely, she thought in dazed misgiving—by what he had done, by the response he had felt in *her*. He took a step back, putting space between them—and a rush of air back into her lungs.

She staggered back, dismayed, as he let her go. He didn't even want to touch her! Was he worried now that she might have read something into his rash kiss? Might even expect something from him as a result, something he had no intention of giving? Damn, damn, *damn*, she fumed silently, unsure whether she was berating him or herself.

'I'm not going to apologise, Sarah. I *wanted* to kiss you.' He reached out to brush her flushed cheek with the tips of his fingers. It was only with a supreme effort that she managed not to react openly to the feathery touch. 'You're very kissable.'

Was he trying to make light of it now? She drew in a ragged breath, feeling confused and shaken but determined not to show it, somehow managing to hide her inner turmoil under a show of haughty indifference.

'You and I, Sarah...we do seem to hit it off. Don't you agree?' As he drawled the words his face twitched in a gesture of impatience. 'What I'm trying to say, Sarah...' He trapped her gaze with the compelling power of his. 'I like you, Sarah, I respect you. I...*trust* you.'

Her stomach clenched. He couldn't seriously be starting to...? No! That was crazy. But he was looking at her so...strangely. With a burning intensity that threatened to pierce right through her defences. She tried not to react to it, tried not to cave in under the sensual spell he was weaving, instead forcing her mind to take control. What did he mean when he said he trusted her? Trusted her not to tell anyone about his rashness a moment ago, his momentary loss of control? Trusted her not to get the wrong idea? Or was he simply saying that he trusted her now...as a friend?

'You've nothing to worry about from me,' she said coolly, her eyes turning to blue ice under his, though her insides were still churning with nervous tension.

He smiled then, one of his rare smiles, reaching his eyes this time, stirring up the very feelings in her that she was fighting to suppress. 'No, I know that, Sarah.' He pressed her hand, and in the brief touch she sensed his relief. 'Come on, we'd better go. I never meant to stay this long. Ten minutes, I intended it to be!'

Ten minutes... Just time to check her flat over, to check *her* over with a few probing questions. Not to get an earful of criticism from her. Not to lose control recklessly and grab her, kiss her.

If he *had* lost control.

She speculated on that as she followed him to his car. Was Kane Brody a man to lose control? She would never have thought so. Not a man of his experience of the world, his strength of character.

Did he regret coming in? He was showing no sign of it. He had an oddly satisfied air about him, she noted in vague bewilderment. And she couldn't shake off the memory of the piercing fire she had seen in his eyes a moment ago, which he had made no attempt to hide. That was what confused her most of all.

She was still puzzling about it when they arrived at his spectacular harbourside house. Was she making a mistake coming here again, getting more deeply involved in his life? It was no use denying that she was strongly attracted to him—much as she might want to pretend otherwise, much as she might fight against it. No other man had ever had this powerful, paralysing effect on her. Kane made her react in a way she had never come near to experiencing before. To go on seeing him, to risk getting more involved with him, would be downright stupidity, playing with fire. What if her feelings got completely out of control? What if she ended up *falling* for him? There was no future for them—none. She would be risking the most fearful heartbreak.

Damn Kane Brody! *Damn* him!

This would have to be the last time she came here, the last time she saw either of them, bitterly painful though it would be. Best to stop it here and now, before she got entangled any further.

'You're very quiet, Sarah,' Kane said as he drove her back to her flat around two o'clock. Today he'd insisted on driving her home himself because he had a meeting to go to in town. Meryl's two boys had gone away on a two-day camp and she was able to stay with Bambi for the rest of the day.

'I've a . . . fair bit on my mind.' Sarah tried to sound detached, tried to *feel* detached, her clear blue eyes fixed to the road in front. She'd had a bitter-sweet couple of hours with Bambi and Kane on their sunny deck overlooking the harbour, enjoying Hilda's tasty quiche and salad lunch while Meryl seized the chance to slip out to do some shopping, leaving them alone. It had been difficult to say goodbye to Bambi, to tell her that she would be going away for a while. Bambi's eyes had blurred with tears, but she had blinked them away and accepted it, as if she had become used to people fading out of her life.

'Tomorrow's my last day at the hospital,' she reminded Kane, keeping her face carefully averted. 'I'm moving out of my flat on Sunday and moving my stuff back home—to my mother's—so I'll have a busy weekend packing up all my things. I won't be needing my flat any more—or a lot of my stuff. Not while I'm working in the outback. And next week, of course, I'm off to the Blue Mountains. I'm really looking forward to having a holiday at last. Two relaxing weeks away! I can hardly wait!' She was piling it on a bit, but pleading lack of time and things to do would make it easier to bow out of his life.

'You have your heart set on going to the Blue Mountains?' Kane asked. His tone was gently mocking, as if he considered the Blue Mountains an insipid choice for a holiday.

'I need the holiday,' she said, her nerves so tense that she found herself almost snapping at him. 'It might not be your idea of a great holiday, but we can't all go jet-setting off overseas whenever we feel like it!'

At once she felt like biting off her tongue. The man didn't deserve to be snarled at. The thought of saying goodbye to him was making her edgy and fractious.

'Sorry,' she mumbled, but he was already drawling a response, showing no signs of taking offence.

'But you'd like to go overseas . . . if you could?'

She glanced at him suspiciously, heat racing along her cheekbones. If he was about to offer her money . . .

'It's not on my agenda at the moment.' Her tone was flat, verging on chilly. 'But I do intend to travel . . . some day. There's plenty of time. I have the rest of my life ahead of me.' How true, she thought, irony curling her lip. The rest of her life to fill . . . somehow.

'You hold a current passport?' he asked.

She compressed her lips, her gaze veering away. 'Why do you ask?'

'*Do* you?' he pressed.

She thought of lying, but couldn't. 'Yes, but I won't be needing——'

'What if *I* needed something?' he cut in.

'You?' Her eyes flickered back to him. What could Kane Brody possibly need? Other than a nanny for his daughter!

'If you're thinking of talking me out of my new nursing job,' she burst out, 'to become Bambi's nanny——'

'You still think that?' Kane brought the Jaguar to a sudden halt, and she realised they were outside her flat already. 'That I've been working up to asking you *that*? Sarah, I told you, nothing could be further from my mind!'

'N-no?' She felt herself flushing, feeling foolish now. She rallied with an effort. 'But you said you needed ... something.'

He shifted in his seat so that he was facing her. 'Sarah, what I need is ... What I'd *like* is to see more of you.' He reached for her hand, capturing it in his.

She felt a prickling heat all over her body and down her limbs. 'Bambi's fine now.' She had to force the words out, acutely aware of the enveloping warmth of his hand over hers, her skin quivering under his touch. 'Really she is.' She didn't dare look at him. 'You don't need a nurse coming in any more.'

'But you're more than a nurse to us, Sarah. You're a friend. A good friend.' His voice was like silken oak, deep and coaxing. 'We both want to see more of you, get to know you even better. We want you to get to know *us* better.'

His cajoling tone was mesmerising her, bewitching her. She had to summon all her will-power to withstand it. She *hated* the weakness he made her feel, resented the fact that he had this power over her. She had to fight it. She had to say no! 'Kane, I don't think I'll have——'

'Time?' he swept in, as if impatient to say what was on his mind. 'Sarah, you would have if you didn't go to the Blue Mountains next week.' Coaxingly, his hand increased its pressure on hers. 'If you came to Italy with Bambi and me instead.'

Her head whipped round, her startled eyes leaping to his. 'If I...*what*?'

'Came to Italy with us.' He turned the full force of his sage-green gaze on her. 'Sarah, I'm tackling this badly, I know. Let me explain. But not here...'

She felt a knot of panic. If he came in to her flat again... If she let his deadly charm weaken her, crumble her defences...

'I thought you had a meeting to go to,' she breathed.

'I do. But it's not until three—the same time that you go on duty, Sarah. I left home early deliberately, to give me time to speak to you. Are you going to let me come in, Sarah?' His voice was low and husky. And dangerously persuasive.

She shook her head. 'Kane, I don't think this is a good idea.' It took a supreme effort to get the words out, an effort to fight him, but she had to, she had to stop this here, now! 'I have my life all mapped out. I've made... plans.' Did her voice sound as thin and piteous to him as it did to her own ears? 'Look... If you need a nanny to go with you to Italy——'

'Damn it, Sarah, I don't need a nanny! Well, not for this trip to Italy. I'll be with Bambi the whole time.'

'A nurse, then.'

'Not a nurse, either, exactly.'

'Then why would you need me to go with you?' Baffled, she eyed him speculatively from under her long lashes. 'Because you feel you owe me something for taking an interest in Bambi?'

'Sarah, it's not——'

'A charitable gesture then, because you feel sorry for me. Because I can't afford the kind of holiday you're used to!' She affected a bantering tone. 'Why not give poor little Sarah a *decent* holiday—all expenses paid...?' Silvery sparks glinted in her eyes, her tone mocking him.

'Obliging Sarah could always give you a hand with Bambi at the same time!'

He looked startled. 'Sarah, you couldn't be more wrong! It's not a debt—*or* a charitable gesture. I'm asking you because I like you and Bambi likes you and we get on so well together. We've *proved* that.'

Proved it? She eyed him warily. What did he mean by that?

At the same time she could feel herself being drawn again into the web of his charm. 'That's very kind of you, Kane—more than kind—but——'

'It doesn't have to interfere with your plans for the future,' he pressed, and she had to fight the dynamic waves of vitality pulsing from him. 'We'll be back in ample time for you to take up your nursing career in the outback. All you'll miss is your holiday in the Blue Mountains...which you can take at any time, can't you? Even outback nurses get leave now and then to come back to civilisation, don't they?'

She sighed, pursing her lips, not answering at once, her mind racing. If he was happy for her to take up her career in the outback, he couldn't be looking for a lengthy relationship with her, either as a friend or as a nanny...let alone as anything more. More? She almost snorted aloud at the thought that he might have anything deeper or more permanent in mind. Men of Kane Brody's ilk looked higher than lowly nurses, nobodies, when they were looking for a long-term partner!

But a short-term fling? Now, that...

Her eyes glinted as she wondered if that was what he had in mind. He might think she fitted the bill nicely. Someone he liked well enough to have a playful fling with, but would never want to get seriously involved with. A career-girl who wouldn't make things difficult for him by stupidly falling in love with him. Someone who rubbed along well with Bambi, and at the same time was medically trained and so would be handy, in the existing circumstances, to have along.

Well, he could forget it! She thrust out her chin. She had no intention of having even a short-lived affair with Kane Brody. The sorry truth was, she wouldn't dare! The violent way her body reacted to him, the dangerous knack he had of draining all her will-power with a mere look, a touch... She shuddered to think what a full-blown affair with him could do to her! She'd sworn long ago never to indulge in an affair unless she was in full control of her emotions. She'd be a fool to...

'Well, Sarah?' His hand touched her arm and she jumped as if burnt. Unnerved, but consciously steeling herself against him, she brought her head round to face him. 'I've already told my friends that I'm coming to the Blue——'

'They'll understand, won't they? How many chances come along for a trip to Italy? First-class travel, all expenses paid!'

She stiffened. 'In my experience, men don't shower women with extravagant gifts without expecting something in return!'

His eyelids flickered under her accusing gaze. Almost... guiltily, she thought, a faint pang quivering through her. She waited stony-faced as he sucked in a deep breath, reaching up to run his long fingers through his hair as if trying to come to some decision.

At length he said, 'Sarah, I won't lie to you. There is a small thing I want in return—I admit it. But it's not what you're thinking.'

What *did* he want? She felt totally bewildered now. Moistening her lips with the tip of her tongue, she asked slowly, 'What is it, Kane, that you want from me?'

His hand dropped to his side. 'Sarah, the reason I'm asking you to come with us to Italy is... Dammit, Sarah, it's because I need your help!'

She frowned at him. 'Then you *do* want my help with Bambi!'

'Sarah, it's... rather more complicated than that.' As he turned the mesmeric force of his gaze on her, his easy assurance seemed to waver, his shoulders lifting and falling in a sigh. 'Hell!' he growled. 'I expected this would be easier.'

She felt a stir of anger. He'd expected her to cave in under his potent charm and jump at his invitation, no questions asked! No doubt he'd expected her to be so overwhelmed by his generosity, his show of interest in her, that she would be ready to promise him anything!

'I'm sorry you're finding it so difficult,' she said stonily. Why should she make it any easier for him? If he wanted something from her, let the arrogant power-house go down on his knees and beg! No doubt that would be a first for Kane Brody!

'Sarah...' He extended his arm, letting his fingers stroke gently down her sleeve. 'I'll need to explain the background first, the lead-up to all this...'

'Kane, just tell me what it is you want from me!' Her patience was at breaking-point, his stroking fingers setting her nerves on edge. She didn't want any lead-up, any background, any distracting smooth talk. She wanted the bottom line, and she wanted it now! 'You can go into the whys and wherefores afterwards.'

'Very well...so long as you'll give me a chance to explain *why* I'm asking this thing of you. It's a big thing, I realise that. Sarah...' His gaze scorched into hers. 'For the duration of our trip to Italy, I want...' He paused, just for a second. 'I want you to pose as my fiancée. As the future Mrs Kane Brody!'

# CHAPTER SIX

SARAH didn't know what she had been expecting, but it certainly wasn't that. For a moment she was speechless. Stunned.

'Now will you let me come in and explain why?' Kane's mouth curved; his tone was sardonic.

Her voice unstuck, the mistrust that had been simmering inside her all along suddenly bubbling up into a red-hot anger and boiling over.

'You've been working up to this from the very beginning, haven't you?' she hissed at him. She was shaking uncontrollably and didn't care if she showed it. 'That swish lunch at Bilson's...the invitations to your home...that—that slimy kiss!' She put all the biting scorn she could muster into her voice.

Giving him no chance to deny it, she accused, 'Everything you did and said was just a shabby ploy to win me over, to make me more malleable to this—this—whatever it is you're up to! Well, you can forget it! And you can get out of my life!' She didn't know what was angering her the most: the thought that his kisses had been nothing but an empty sham, or the fact that he'd used her, that all the attention and flattery he'd been showering on her had simply been a means of softening her up.

'Sarah, I had to be sure we could get along... And that kiss... I *wanted* to kiss you. I *enjoyed* it.'

She didn't believe him. All along he'd been playing on her sympathy for Bambi, and on his seductive power as a man, to get her to the point where he thought he could sweep in triumphantly for the kill.

'You're a ruthless, contemptible, cold-blooded fraud!' she spat at him, wrenching around to claw at the door-handle.

Kane's hand closed on her arm. 'Sarah, please at least let me explain *why* I'm asking this of you. It's important, believe me. Bambi's future could depend on it.'

'Bambi?' She paused, turning slowly back to face him, her face tight with mistrust. 'All right. Tell me,' she grated. '*Now*. Why are you so in need of a make-believe fiancée?' Her tone was derisive, her eyes like shards of ice. Inwardly, her mind was tumbling with possible answers. Something to do with his hot-shot business, no doubt! The need to swing some important financial deal in Italy, which if successful would ensure Bambi's future. Having a fiancée by his side would give the impression that he was the steady, reliable type. Ha!

Or—her mouth dipped in scorn—maybe he wanted to get some woman off his back. Though she failed to see how *that* would affect Bambi's future, unless the woman was making a nuisance of herself.

Kane's voice cut into her thoughts. 'I need Bambi's grandparents to believe I'm getting married again,' he said baldly, wasting no time leading up to the point. 'They're the sole reason Bambi and I are going to Italy— to pay them a promised visit.'

She took a moment to take it in. It was only the thought of Bambi, the other pawn in Kane Brody's little game, that made her sit quietly and listen.

'When my wife died, her parents, Antonio and Maria Corbelli, flew out here from Italy for her funeral.' Kane's voice held no emotion. None. If the memory of that tragic time still tormented him, he didn't show it by so much as a flicker, his face seeming carved from stone.

She sat silently, waiting for him to go on.

'They were devastated, as you can imagine, at losing their daughter. They wanted to take Bambi, our daughter—*Claudia's* daughter, they persisted in calling her—back with them to Italy, to bring her up themselves, with Bambi's aunts and uncles and cousins.' His voice had turned harsh, the cynical lines slashing deep into his cheeks. 'They felt she would be better off with them there, in a close family environment, than here with me, her father.'

'But that's——'

'Wrong?' His mouth twisted. 'Oh, legally they knew they had no hope of winning custody, but morally they felt they had every right to her, that it would be in Bambi's best interests. They accused me of putting my business interests ahead of my family... reminding me that I had often left my wife to cope alone with Bambi while I was away. Which I could hardly deny. It's inevitable in the business I'm in.'

'You...go away a lot?' Sarah ventured, and had a sudden vision of his small daughter's big pensive eyes. Poor Bambi. Since her mother had died she would have been left at home all alone, with only a nanny or some other carer for solace.

'My job entails frequent travel out of town and interstate—if only for a day or two at a time—and the odd overseas trip,' Kane rapped back. 'My wife and child often travelled with me. When that was impossible, they were more than adequately cared for. My wife always had household staff and nannies to help her.' His mouth tightened. 'Despite what my in-laws might think, I have never put my business ahead of my family.'

'And...what about now?' Sarah couldn't hold back the question. 'Do you still go away a lot and leave Bambi at home?' At home with the household staff and the nannies!

Kane's eyes pierced hers, the steely grey more pronounced than the green in the dimness of the car's interior. 'I keep my time away from home to a minimum,' he said curtly. Plainly, he didn't relish having his actions questioned by an outsider. The grandparents might have the right to do it, but he had no intention of taking it from Sarah Vane!

'However,' he conceded in the same biting tone, 'Bambi's grandparents don't agree. They feel my daughter is missing out and accuse me of neglecting her.

That's why they want her to go and live with them. I will never allow it,' he vowed, with a grating harshness that sent a shiver down Sarah's spine.

'And yet,' she said slowly, 'you've agreed to go and visit them?'

'It was a promise I made at my wife's funeral. Maria and Antonio wanted to take Bambi back to Italy with them at the time, but I refused to let them, even for a holiday. I didn't trust them.' His brow lowered. 'Anyway, I felt it was important that Bambi be with me at that time...that she suffer as little disruption as possible. The Corbellis tried every argument in the book,' he ground out, 'refusing at first to go back without her. To get rid of them, I made a promise to bring Bambi over to Italy for her fourth birthday—her third I considered too close. The family will be on vacation when Bambi's birthday falls at the end of this month. They'll be staying at their summer villa on Lake Como in northern Italy.'

'I see,' Sarah said slowly. 'And you want them to believe that you're getting married again, and giving Bambi a mother and a normal family life...so that they'll get off your back!' She couldn't hide the censure in her voice.

'That's about it.'

'But, Kane, surely they'll find out eventually that you've lied to them, when they learn that you didn't get married after all?'

He didn't turn a hair. 'Engagements get broken all the time. And even if they do suspect later that it was all a set-up, they won't find out until we're safely back home in Australia—and it will be too late then. It's only while we're in Italy that Bambi will be...vulnerable.'

'Vulnerable?'

'Sarah, I know this family. As long as they see Bambi as a poor motherless waif, and me as a business-obsessed single parent, they'll try to keep her there...somehow. They might even try to...spirit her away somewhere out of sight, hoping I'll be so keen to get back to my precious business——' his lip curled in scorn '—that I'll throw in the towel and come back without her.'

She gaped at him. 'You actually believe ... they'd try to *kidnap* her?'

'They wouldn't see it as kidnapping.'

'But the authorities——'

'Sarah, the Corbellis are a very powerful family in Italy. A big banking family, with branches all over the country. The authorities over there would be on their side. They'd close their eyes, look the other way. They'd never help me. A foreigner.'

'But what about the authorities here in Australia? Bambi's an Australian citizen, isn't she? They'd have to help you. You're Bambi's father!'

'Sarah, I'm not going to put Bambi through the trauma of a custody battle, even one I'd be assured of winning. Or through any kind of tug-of-war, for that matter. Bambi means everything to me. I won't see her hurt. And I don't intend to lose her. Believe me, Sarah, this is the best way. With you there, playing the part of Bambi's future mother—and you'll do it well, Sarah—they're hardly likely to try anything.' His gaze clamped on hers. 'Are you going to help me or not?'

She didn't flinch under the pressure. 'Wouldn't it be better and more convincing all round to take a *real* fiancée with you?' She pressed home her point before he could speak. 'I'm sure the great Kane Brody would have no trouble finding a woman—the right woman, I mean—to fill the gap in your life ... and in your daughter's. You can't deny that there *is* a gap—or you wouldn't be proposing that I fill it, even if it is only temporarily. Your daughter *needs* a mother, Kane—a real mother! It's not fair to her to——'

'It won't affect her—she's too young to understand,' he sliced in over her. 'And as for her needing a mother...' His tone was scathing. 'She has a father. She doesn't need anyone else. And I don't need a wife!'

'You may think that now——'

'I won't change my mind.' An implacable statement of fact.

She sighed. 'But, Kane, why *me*? A virtual stranger, an unknown. I don't even move in the same circles you do. None of your friends or colleagues know me from a bar of soap!'

'They won't need to. This is purely a short-term business arrangement for the duration of our trip to Italy,' he said with ruthless candour. 'Believe me, Sarah, it's best this way. For both of us. Besides,' he added, as if realising how cold-blooded he'd made it sound, 'the women who move in my...circles, as you put it, leave me cold, quite frankly. Scratch the surface charm and the good looks, and you'll find they're all self-centred, calculating little gold-diggers underneath!'

How jaded and cynical he was! She shook her head at him. His wife must have been someone very special, very dear to him, to show up all other women since in such a degrading light. Or was it simply that the women he'd met since had thrown themselves at him with such voracious enthusiasm that they'd sent him running for cover?

'And how do you know that I'm not...like them?' she taunted softly. 'Aren't you afraid——' her eyes flared a roguish challenge '—that I might sue you afterwards for breach of promise?'

'Try it, and you'll wish you'd never been born!'

The violence of his reaction shook her. Incensed that he'd taken her playful taunt seriously, she regarded him with a dangerous glitter in her eye. 'Is that a reaction from bitter experience? I've heard there *are* men who propose marriage to get what they want from a woman! Tell me,' she said disparagingly, 'how many breach of promise suits have you been subjected to in the past couple of years?'

For a moment she thought he was going to grab her by the throat and throttle her. As it was, his fingers dug so deeply into her arm that she winced. But he brought himself under control, loosening his grip and raking her coldly with his eyes.

'None,' he bit out. 'Nor am I likely to be. I wouldn't be fool enough to get myself into that position. However, you've made your point,' he grated. 'You drive a hard bargain, Sarah Vane. I thought a free trip overseas would have been enough to satisfy you.'

She tensed as he drew back his hand, gulping as he plunged it into his pocket. 'OK, you win,' he rasped, pulling out his wallet. 'Ten thousand dollars—five in advance, another five at the end of our arrangement.'

She gaped at him, quivering with barely contained outrage. 'Is that what you're used to doing? Buying women off?' She clenched her hands into white-knuckled fists. 'You really don't think much of women, do you, Kane Brody?'

He didn't deny it. 'Most women, I've found,' he ground out, languidly fingering the wallet in his hand, 'want something in return for their favours. Some are quite modest in their demands, settling for opening nights, or flowers, or being wined and dined in style. Others won't be content with anything less than dia-monds—or cold, hard cash.'

'You can't be . . . serious?' But she could tell by the sneer on his lips that he was. 'Well,' she said, this time managing to throw open her door, 'you won't need to buy *me*. I wouldn't touch your money!' She looked pity-ingly into his face. 'I'm sorry you have such a low opinion of women, Kane. I feel sorry for you!'

'Don't be!' he lashed back. He didn't believe her, ob-viously. 'I'm not complaining. I'm prepared to pay their price if I want their company. It means I don't have to offer them anything more . . . personal. Like a piece of myself!'

She shook her head at him as she swung her legs out of the car. 'Surely you would rather have a woman who would——' she shrugged '—just want you for yourself?'

The cynicism etched in his face deepened. 'Such a woman doesn't exist.'

'You mean...' She hesitated before asking, 'You feel that no other woman can ever live up to the memory of...your wife?'

'Let's leave my wife out of this!' he rasped, as if he couldn't bear to talk about his wife and other women in the same breath. His eyes snapped to his watch. 'You'd better go and get ready for work.' He reached for her arm, his eyes searching hers. 'Sarah, I know I'm asking a lot of you. But...come to Italy with us. Please.' His voice had lost its harsh edge, and the urgency, the magnetic appeal in his eyes was hard to resist. 'Lake Como is a very beautiful place—especially at this time of year.'

She flicked her tongue over her lips. 'I——'

'For Bambi's sake.'

Her eyes wavered under his. He knew how to get to her! 'If I agree, it will be *purely* for Bambi's sake, I promise you!' she said loftily. 'Let me sleep on it,' she added, but she knew her answer already, and so, she sensed when he gave an infinitesimal nod, did he.

As she climbed out he jumped out too, and strode round to offer her a helping hand. '*Should* you accept, Sarah——' arrogantly assuming that she would '—I'll want you to spend some more time with us before we leave. With no hospital to go to next week, you'll be free, I trust, to spend your evenings with us—Bambi and me. You can use the daytime to do whatever one needs to do to prepare for a week overseas.'

She tilted her chin. 'You're assuming——'

'I'm counting on you, Sarah,' he amended smoothly. 'We need your help.' As she turned away he said, 'Don't bother to buy any new clothes for the trip. Just take enough to get you there.' She paused, a question in her eyes. 'We'll shop when we get to Milan,' he said. 'We'll rest up there overnight before driving to Lake Como. Your wardrobe, I must insist, will be my responsibility. Both the choice and the cost.'

To ensure that she was suitably rigged out to play the part of the future Mrs Kane Brody? Sarah's eyes flared, and then narrowed. Very well, Kane Brody, she thought. You want this to be purely a business arrangement. I'll treat it as one.

'By all means,' she agreed calmly. 'On condition that at the end of our trip you'll take your fine clothes back. *I'll* have no further need of them. I'm sure you have women-friends who will be only too delighted to take them off your hands!'

He eyed her speculatively for a moment, then spread his hands. 'If that's your condition, Sarah...I accept. We'll be flying out next Friday—a week from today. I trust that will give you enough time to prepare?'

'*If* I accept, I'm sure it will.' Let him stew overnight. He deserved it!

She swung away.

'Sarah?'

Again she paused, glancing round with a sigh. 'Yes?'

'Think about my other offer.' He patted his wallet. 'It still stands. I'll ring you in the morning.'

She was seething as she left him. He still thought he had to offer an inducement, that the overseas trip and a new Italian wardrobe wouldn't be enough to satisfy her! What in the world, she wondered, could have given him such a low opinion of women?

She sighed, and shook her head. His wife Claudia must have been a saint, a veritable angel to have made all other women suffer so much by comparison.

Sarah wondered where the week had gone. It had flown by. A busy week, emotionally charged at times. Explaining her overseas trip to her mother—after she had let Kane know she would go, stressing again that it was purely for Bambi's sake—was just one of the things she'd had to do.

'You're going to *Italy*? With Kane Brody? *The* Kane Brody?' Speculation had leapt to Laura Vane's eyes.

Sarah was quick to dampen her mother's enthusiasm, explaining that it was simply a job, that she was going with the Brody family purely as a nurse, to keep an eye on Kane Brody's daughter Bambi, who had been a special patient of hers. She had stressed that Mr Brody, as she primly referred to him, was merely employing her for the duration of the trip, and that on her return home she still intended to go ahead with her plans to join the flying doctor service.

A sigh escaped her mother's lips. 'You're turning into a real career-woman, Sarah. And heaven knows why you have to bury yourself in the outback. It's so far away, so remote from everything and everybody. What sort of life will you have out there? You'll never meet anybody. And I—I'll never see you!'

'Of course you'll see me, Mum. I'll have holidays,' Sarah had soothed, stifling a faint sigh. She loved her mother, but she could only take her in small doses. At close quarters, for any length of time, Laura tended to be clingy, stifling—always had done. 'I'm looking forward to it,' she assured her mother. 'And of course I'll meet people, Mum. Lots of people. It'll be fun. A challenge. I'll be doing something useful. Helping people.'

'You're twenty-six years old, Sarah. You should be thinking of getting married and——'

'Mum!' Sarah's voice was sharper than she intended. Her mother, above everyone, should understand, but she didn't, she wouldn't. She'd put on blinkers and simply refused to face the fact that marriage and motherhood, for her daughter, would be recklessly unwise—if not a tragic mistake. Sarah, not wanting to cause her mother further distress by railing at her fate, had put on a brave face, assuring her mother over and over that marriage and a family weren't what she wanted from life, that her nursing career was all she wanted. She'd even managed to convince herself, burying her own regrets and subli-mating her love and need for children of her own into caring for the children of others—children in need of a nurse's special care. And she was happy. Well, happy enough.

Facing her mother, she used the argument she'd used many times before. 'Mum, you know I'm not the domestic type. I don't *want* to get married. Nursing is my life. You'll just have to accept it!'

'But, dear——'

'Mum, I have to fly. I need to do some shopping before I go to the Brodys' for dinner. See you!'

It was Wednesday night, only two nights before they were due to leave, that turned out to be the low point of the week. And she had no one to blame but herself.

After reading Bambi a bedtime story and then kissing her goodnight, she stood back to let Kane Brody take her place at the bedside and spend a few moments alone with his daughter. Before leaving the room she paused, watching pensively as Kane tucked the child in and bent down to kiss her, lightly brushing his lips to hers.

As he straightened and followed Sarah out, he caught her eye. 'What's wrong? Why are you looking at me like that?'

She looked up at him uncertainly.

'Well?' Grasping her arm none too gently, Kane steered her into his exquisite white lounge. 'You have something on your mind, Sarah. What is it?'

She looked up at him. 'Kane...' She hesitated.

'Let's hear it!'

She swallowed. 'Kane, I know that you love your daughter. And you *show* her you love her...in many different ways. At night you ask after her day and you make sure she has a toy to cuddle, and you tuck her in and you kiss her goodnight. But, Kane...sometimes a child needs more.'

'More?' His eyes were cold, his voice strained. 'If you mean a mother——'

'No!' she cried. 'I wasn't thinking of... Well, of course, it would be wonderful if Bambi had a mother, naturally it would...and brothers and sisters. But I'm not thinking of—well—of what might happen in the future. I'm thinking of *now*. Of what she needs *now*.'

'What *does* she need now?' His tone was wary now, aloof. Obviously he thought he was already giving his child all she needed. His love, his care, his protection, and all the toys and material things she could possibly want.

'I think she would like it if you held her in your arms now and then and gave her a cuddle. A real bear-hug, I mean. And maybe if you kissed her occasionally, at other times than just at bedtime. Like her mother would have done. And if you encouraged her to hug and cuddle *you*, the way she hugs and cuddles...Oogly.'

She gulped, trying not to flinch from him in the heavy silence that followed her brave words. Kane was the one who finally broke it. 'I've noticed how fond she is of that odd-looking toy.' His words came slowly, as if dragged from him. 'I never see her hugging any of the dolls *I've* given her.'

She shot him a look of sympathy. 'Maybe they're just not as cuddly as Oogly,' she said lightly. 'Or maybe,' she added carefully, 'she simply relates better to Oogly. I did tell her he needs lots of cuddles. Kane, I think *she* needs them too.'

When he didn't say anything, she ventured, 'If Bambi doesn't cuddle the dolls you've given her, Kane, maybe it's her way of telling you she'd rather be cuddling *you*.'

'Hmm,' he said non-committally. After another long pause, he muttered, 'You think so, do you? Your experience as a children's nurse has given you an insight into what makes all children tick?'

'Kane, please don't take this the——'

His hand waved her into silence. 'I haven't taken offence, Sarah. On the contrary, I find your candour refreshing. I don't often see it. When I do, it's seldom given with your sensitivity, and only succeeds in rubbing me up the wrong way. I know you have Bambi's welfare in mind. You have no selfish motive of your own, no hidden agenda—which is why I chose you, Sarah, for this trip to Italy. Because I know you care. You're doing this for us, not for any future reward for yourself.'

And because, Kane Brody, Sarah reflected with a flash of insight of a different kind, which brought with it a faint pang, I'm not a threat to you. You can feel confident that I won't expect anything of you...afterwards.

'Anything else you feel I should be doing differently?' Kane challenged with a faint twist of his lips. 'If you have, let's hear it now, *before* we go to Italy. I don't want to give my in-laws any more ammunition to fire at me.'

His in-laws! So that was why he'd heard her out so patiently. For his daughter's sake he'd be prepared to listen to anything, to *do* anything, she suspected, to hold on to her.

She resolved to put him to the test.

'Kane...you always avoid talking about Bambi's mother. Your...wife. You never talk about her...to Bambi.'

At once his face hardened, the green eyes changing to grey ice. 'My wife is dead. You know that. Let her rest in peace.'

'But are *you* at peace, Kane? Is Bambi?' Her concern for them both emboldened her to press on. 'Maybe you both *need* to talk—to grieve openly. It's often the——'

'Leave it, Sarah.' The coldness in his voice chilled her. But what, she wondered in swift sympathy, lay behind that icy coldness? Unresolved pain? Anger? Even guilt, perhaps? Festering like a sore inside him?

Surely blotting it out wasn't the way to deal with it.

'Kane, I'm sorry. I'm causing you pain. But I'm thinking of Bambi.' *And* of you, she thought. 'I know you've lost your wife...but Bambi has lost her mother too. She's only a child. She can't understand, or explain how she feels. But she must miss her mother terribly.

And wonder *why* she's gone. She might even be blaming herself . . .'

'Bambi was only two and a half when my wife died,' Kane said tonelessly. 'She was too young to realise what had happened. Or even to remember or mourn her mother for long.'

'Oh, Kane, are you sure? Babies less than a year old know and recognise their mothers. They fret when they go away, even for a few hours. Or even when they just lose sight of them for a few minutes.'

'Bambi has always had nannies, even when my wife was alive, so she had a buffer when her mother died.' Kane's voice was harsh now, dismissive. 'She might have missed her initially, but she was soon over it. She had others to take her mother's place.'

How cold and callous he sounded! Was it, Sarah wondered, his way of masking his own grief?

'But no one constant . . . except you,' she persisted gently. And even you're not there all the time, she thought. You have to leave her each day to go to work. And sometimes you have to go away overnight . . . or for longer.

A shadow, almost a scowl, crossed his face. 'Plenty of parents go to work each day and leave their children with caretakers.'

Was he regretting now that he'd encouraged her to speak up? Despite a growing misgiving, she forced herself to go on. 'Kane, my point is . . . Bambi must still wonder about her mother. Wonder if she's gone for good or if she's going to come back one day, or even if *she* could be to blame for her mother going away. Not talking about her will only make her wonder and worry more—especially when she meets other children who do have mothers. Have you told her about the accident, Kane? About what happened? And told her honestly that her mother will never be coming back?'

'She knows enough. For now.' He was getting annoyed. It was in the grim line of his mouth, in the ominous darkening of his brow. 'She knows that her mother's gone away and won't be coming back. She's accepted that. She's never asked for her, never cried for her. She's over it, Sarah.'

Sarah sighed. Poor Bambi! Kane was deluding himself—she was sure of it. She made one last appeal to him. 'Kane, she doesn't show it because she's bottled it all up inside. It's not even been two years. She must still remember her, still miss her...miss not having a mother who's there all the time. And she must wonder why she hasn't. Kane, if you don't talk to her about it,' she warned, 'your wife's family *will*. What's to stop them saying something while we're over there? It could come as a terrible shock to Bambi, hearing it from them and not from you. Would you want that?'

He brushed a hand across his mouth. That point, obviously, had given him pause for thought.

She pressed home her advantage. 'Tell her what happened, Kane. Stress that it was an accident, and reassure her, let her know that it wasn't her fault. And that you're here for her, and always will be. If she cries, encourage it. And give her the kisses and cuddles she's not getting any longer from her mother. She needs them badly. Not from me, Kane. Not from Oogly. From *you*.'

'Damn it, Sarah, what do you know?' In a sudden violent movement, he crashed his fist into the palm of his hand. 'How do you know my daughter was getting kisses and cuddles from her mother? How do you know she misses her, or that I miss her, or how we feel? You don't know! You can't! You don't know anything about it!'

She staggered back, shaken by his fury. 'Kane, I'm sorry! I—I just assumed... You mean you don't miss her? You d-didn't love your wife?' Was that what he was saying?

He threw up his hands. 'Sarah, none of this is any of your business. I know you mean well, but this particular topic is taboo. Is that clear? And don't start speculating or assuming—it won't get you anywhere!' He grabbed her by the shoulders and gave her a shake. 'And don't go off with the idea that I didn't love my wife. I did. I loved her to distraction. Does that answer your question?'

His face was a breath away from hers, the ferocity in his eyes frightening her, rendering her speechless for a second. What had she said to set him off like this? What chord had she touched? If only she had minded her own business! Well, she would in future. She certainly would.

Gulping, she forced herself to speak. 'I'd better be getting home. I've had a long day.' She had brought her own car this evening, thank heaven, so wasn't relying on Kane to drive her home. Would she see him again tomorrow night, as previously understood? Or...ever?

After this, would he still want her going to Italy with him?

# CHAPTER SEVEN

SARAH kept herself busy the next morning, helping her mother round the house, trying not to think of Kane or whether her trip to Italy was on or off. Last night when they'd parted he had simply said, 'I'll call you tomorrow,' not I'll *see* you tomorrow. It seemed an ominous sign.

It was only as she was clearing away the lunch dishes that the phone rang at last. She dived for it, reaching it a second before her mother.

'Hello.' Her hand, she realised, was trembling.

'Sarah, good day. Kane Brody.'

She took a deep breath. 'Hello, Kane. How are you?' She spoke carefully, expecting the worst.

'Sarah, sorry I snapped your head off last night. I hope you haven't changed your mind about coming with us tomorrow?'

She let her breath out in a sigh. He still wanted her to go with them! A frown followed the sigh. Because he needed her help—that was the only reason. She felt a mixed reaction, part-relief, part-hostility. Would he be apologising if he didn't want something from her?

'No, I haven't changed my mind,' she said, keeping her tone coolly impersonal. 'I'm sorry too. I had no right to speak out the way I did. I promise you it won't happen again.'

'Sarah, I might not have liked what I heard, but it sank in. And made sense.'

It obviously wasn't easy for him to admit it. Of course—her lip gave a wry twitch—he was only backing down because she was vital to his plans.

'I stayed at home this morning with Bambi.' His tone was as impassive as hers. 'We talked. About her mother.'

98

Though he didn't go into details, she sensed instinctively that it must have been torrid, even traumatic. For both of them.

'Kane, I hope it didn't...' She couldn't hardly put it into words. Had it made things better... or worse?

'No, she's fine. I'd say it's helped, if anything.' Cool, clipped statements, keeping any emotion under tight control.

'I'm glad.' She felt her tense muscles relaxing, her spirits lifting, his cautious admission bringing a lump to her throat.

'You're still coming over for dinner tonight?' He shot the question at her. 'It'll be our last chance to get together before our flight tomorrow.'

'All right. If you think——'

'I do. Got a little black dress?'

'I have, as it happens.'

'Wear it tonight. We'll put Bambi to bed early and have a special dinner, just the two of us. Come at six. We won't make it a late night in case you want to do some last-minute packing.'

He wasn't expecting any argument, and she gave him none.

'I'll be there,' was all she said. This is a job, a business arrangement, she reminded herself. These evenings with Bambi, the mock engagement we're planning, even this intimate dinner of Kane's this evening—they're just a necessary lead-up, a part of the job. So treat it like a job. Don't start looking for anything deeper, more personal in all this. You won't find it.

And it was for the best. Looking on it purely as a job would make it easier. Easier all round.

Almost as soon as she stepped into the Brody house she sensed the subtle change in Bambi, the shy blossoming, like a timid tortoise emerging from its shell. The child was definitely more at ease with her father, more openly affectionate, even winding her arms round him on a couple of occasions for a kiss and a cuddle which he, Sarah noted with a gulp of emotion, gave back in full measure.

She found herself smiling as Kane swung the child into the air after one of their hugs and spun her around, making the little girl laugh aloud and squeal in delight, something Sarah had never heard her do before. And Kane even laughed aloud himself, and growled like a bear, showing a side of him she wouldn't have believed existed.

At bedtime Bambi produced a silver-framed photograph to show Sarah, proudly announcing, 'This is my mummy.'

Gazing down at the photograph, Sarah saw the ravishingly beautiful face of Claudia Brody for the first time.

'You have your mummy's beautiful dark eyes,' she said carefully, conscious of Kane's presence in the room. 'And the same dark wavy hair.' But Bambi was a softer version of her mother, lacking the—what was it?—the flamboyance, the brilliance, the dramatic air of the woman in the photograph.

'My mummy's dead,' the child said solemnly. 'She was in a bad acc-i-dent.' She seemed proud of herself for getting her tongue around the word. 'Mummy's car was going too fast and it crashed. But she didn't feel anything,' she added quickly, not wanting Sarah to feel that she had. 'It happened too quickly. My mummy's gone.' She looked up at Sarah, her eyes huge and blurring now with tears. She bravely blinked them away. 'But she's still watching over me. Like God does. She still loves me.'

'Oh, yes, she still loves you,' Sarah agreed, misty-eyed herself as she instinctively reached out to stroke the child's soft hair. 'Just as your daddy does.' She couldn't quite look at Kane, unsure of how he was taking this frank talk about his wife.

'Well, now, how about putting Mummy's photograph back next to that photograph of you?' Kane's voice intruded. 'It's time you were in bed asleep.'

'I'll put it next to that photograph of you and me, Daddy.' Bambi smiled up at him, not wanting him to be left out.

'All right, honey. With the photograph of you and me,' Kane agreed gruffly.

Talking about his wife is still tough for him, Sarah thought, as the child put the photograph back and climbed into bed, but he's making an effort, for his daughter's sake.

Was it helping him too, she wondered hopefully, finally to be able to talk about his wife, and openly display photographs of her? Bottling up his grief, denying it, surely couldn't be the way to resolve it.

She had come dressed this evening as Kane had decreed, in a simple black dress that skimmed over her slender curves, and sheer dark stockings showing her long legs to full advantage. She had no idea yet what Kane had in mind for their 'special' dinner. He'd said nothing about taking her out, and who would mind Bambi if he did? Kane had already dismissed Hilda for the evening and the housekeeper had retired to her room, so he certainly wasn't expecting Hilda to keep an eye on his daughter—or to cook dinner. And there was nobody else in the kitchen cooking, as far as she knew. It was a puzzle.

A knock on the door solved the mystery. Kane had engaged Sydney's top catering firm to deliver a romantic dinner for two to his home. Sparkling silver, gleaming crystal, and finely embroidered table-mats quickly transformed the polished dining-room table, with fresh yellow roses and long candles adding a romantic finishing touch. Smoked salmon and caviare materialised, and the finest French wines. A main course of poached coral trout with a lobster sauce and baby vegetables followed, with hazelnut parfait topped with pistachio sauce making a mouth-watering finish. Kane was a perfect host, charming and attentive.

After coffee had been brought in and the caterers had packed up and left, Kane steered Sarah into the lounge and stood her in front of the circular wall-mirror.

'Wait right there,' he said, and stepped away for a moment. Moving back to stand behind her, he draped an exquisite diamond-encrusted pearl necklace round her slender throat. A shiver rippled down Sarah's spine at the touch of his warm fingers at her nape as he secured the clasp.

'Like it?' he asked, his hands sliding to her shoulders.

She had never seen anything more beautiful. But——

'Kane, you didn't have to wine and dine me to make me agree to wear this. You only had to ask.' She spoke coolly—more coolly than she felt. 'I know it's only a prop—so that I can play my part more convincingly in front of your wife's family.'

His fingers tensed on her shoulders. 'It's not a prop, Sarah. I don't want it back...afterwards. I want you to keep it.'

She flinched. Another pay-off? 'Don't be silly, Kane,' she said, swinging round to face him, so that he had to let her go. 'I wouldn't *want* to keep it. I'll have no use for diamonds and pearls where I'm going.'

'You won't always be in the outback, Sarah. Keep it for when you come back. I want you to.'

'Thank you, Kane, that's more than generous...but no. I'm prepared to play the part you want me to play without unnecessary...bribes. Either diamonds or——' she waved a hand towards the dining-room '—French champagne and caviare!'

A baffled frown creased his brow. 'You're saying you didn't enjoy our dinner?'

'It enjoyed it very much,' she said, and thought, I would have enjoyed it a lot more if you'd wined and dined me simply because you wanted my company. But she kept the thought to herself, not wanting him to think she was eager for *his* company! Damn it—she wasn't!

'But you think I had an ulterior motive,' he said flatly. 'Sarah, it was nothing like that. I thought you'd *like* a special dinner, a chance to dress up and be pampered a bit. My... wife loved all that stuff. She *expected* it.'

'Kane, I'm not your wife. Or even your wife-to-be. I'm just playing a role, remember? It's difficult enough. Don't make it any more difficult for me!'

He shook his head in exasperation. 'I don't understand you, Sarah. You're not like other women. None that I've ever known.'

No, she thought, stung, I'm not. I'm well aware that I'm not one of your classy sophisticates.

'Having second thoughts, are you,' she asked with bitter-edged sweetness, 'about whether I'm suitable for the role of your fiancée?' Her eyes narrowed, flickering under his. 'I think,' she said slowly, 'I'm beginning to understand. Tonight was just a test, wasn't it? To see how I'd measure up in the glamorous world you're about to plunge me into! You wanted to make sure I'd fit into it—use the right fork, perhaps, look the part, hold an intelligent conversation—before it was too late!'

'Damn it, Sarah!' His hand shot out to grip her arm. 'You don't think much of me, do you? You couldn't be further off the mark! I simply wanted to give you a special dinner, to spoil you a bit. As a way of saying thank you for what you've agreed to do. Don't go looking for hidden motives,' he growled, 'because you won't find them!'

'All right!' she gasped, trying to shake off his hand. 'You can let me go! *Thank* you!' Released, she took a step back, and bit her lip, ashamed now of her outburst. 'Kane, I'm sorry. I... over-reacted. It's been a lovely evening—perfect.' And it *had*. 'I'm sorry if I've spoilt it for you.'

'You haven't.'

He wouldn't admit it if she had—not with so much at stake. She stepped back quickly, out of his reach. 'I'd better go. I still have some packing to do and I don't want a late night. I'll...see you tomorrow.'

She left him and fled to her car.

It was evening when they arrived in Milan after the long flight from Sydney, via Singapore and Frankfurt. A taxi whisked them from the airport to the central city hotel which Kane had booked for the night. The long flight, despite the luxury and comfort of their first-class seats, had left them weary and in need of a soft bed for the night, and that was where they headed, as soon as Kane had deposited Sarah in her luxurious room down the passage from his own two-bedroomed suite, which he was sharing with his daughter.

'I'll order breakfast sent up to you in the morning,' were his parting words. 'Come to my room when you're ready—say, around nine—and we'll go shopping.'

'Milan is not like other cities in Italy,' Kane said as they strolled along the sun-drenched streets. 'It's faster, smarter, more modern. Rome and Florence and Venice live mostly for the past, but Milan is very much today's city—more European, in a way, than Italian. It's a major financial centre. And of course——' he looked down at her '—the fashion centre of the world.'

'Yes, so I've heard.' Sarah flicked her tongue over her lips. Fashion was the reason they were spending the next few hours here in Milan instead of driving straight to Lake Como. Kane might have fooled the Corbelli family into believing they needed some breathing time to unwind after their long trip, but the prime reason, the true reason they were here, was to transform Sarah Vane into an elegant fiancée worthy of the great Kane Brody.

Already she was wearing his ring—a fine antique diamond and sapphire ring which, Kane had told her, had been in his family for generations. He'd presented it to her without fuss or fanfare before they'd left the hotel.

With Bambi trotting between them, they wandered the length of the elegant Via Monte Napolitano, lined on both sides with exclusive fashion boutiques. Sarah caught the names on the shop-fronts. Ungaro, Valentino, Gucci, Armani... Her mind reeled. All the top Italian fashion designers were represented here. And the prices—the ones displayed in the windows—were mind-boggling.

'You're very quiet, Sarah.' Kane tilted his head at her. 'You don't seem overly excited at being in the fashion centre of the world. I thought high fashion was a turn-on for women.'

'You have quite a few false assumptions about women,' she heard herself almost snapping at him. 'I realise I'm not in the same league as the ultra-sophisticates you normally mix with, but not all women think only about French champagne and designer clothes!' She sucked in her breath. 'I—I'm sorry,' she was quick to retract. 'I'm a bit tense, I guess. About—about...' She looked helplessly down at the ring on her finger.

He touched her arm, his fingers bringing a prickling warmth to her skin. 'No need to apologise, Sarah. You're right—there are other things in life. For a lot of women. I'd forgotten there *are* women like you.'

She turned away to hide the quick flush that spread over her cheeks, shaken for a second by the intensity in his voice. But only for a second. Don't be fooled, Sarah, she cautioned herself. Kane Brody's a very clever man, a man of vast experience with women. A devious man too, devious enough to suggest this risky masquerade in the first place.

'Now, Sarah...' A sardonic smile touched Kane's lips. 'You'll let me choose for you.' His fingers trailed down her arm. There was arrogance and a steely undercurrent in his voice.

At once her anger flared again, the brush of his fingers setting her nerve-ends on edge. 'Oh, don't worry, you won't have to twist my arm. If you believe that the only way you can fool your in-laws into accepting me as your fiancée is to fork out the national debt to make me presentable, go ahead—it's your money!'

His fingers closed over her wrist. 'I thought you'd *want* to wear this stuff. I thought all women dreamed of getting decked out in Ungaros and Valentinos. My wife certainly did!'

At the mention of his wife her anger subsided, her blue eyes shimmering under his. She was beginning to understand. He wasn't trying to bring her up to scratch, to cast her in the same mould as the other women who moved in his elegant circles. He genuinely believed he was giving her what he thought every woman craved!

'Kane...' She hesitated. She was here to do a job, she had to remember, to play a part, not to get on her high horse. 'I just ask that you let me be *me*,' she pleaded. 'When I wear something, I need to feel right. I don't want to face your in-laws pretending to be someone I'm not.'

'What I choose will be right for you, Sarah,' he said with an arrogance that brooked no argument. 'Leave it to me. And, Sarah?' He paused, his hand still gripping her wrist, his other clasping his daughter's tiny hand. 'It will work out, I promise you. You'll see it through...admirably.'

She gulped. 'I hope so.'

'Sure you will. You're a clever, sensible woman, Sarah, and you're marvellous with Bambi. And you and I...' His eyes pinned hers for a long second. 'We rub along well enough to fool these people. And we both know there's no danger of complicating it with any...emotional involvement.'

She stiffened, resentment flaring that he still thought it necessary to remind her that this was only a job. Not to get any ideas. Not to expect anything...afterwards.

She was to back out gracefully at the end of this masquerade and go her own way, leaving Kane and Bambi to go theirs.

He should know he was safe, damn him! She stifled an odd little pang. If he only knew how safe he really was!

'We'll start here,' said Kane, glancing round at the stylish window behind them. 'What you'll need is some casual holiday gear, suitable for summer on the lake, and one or two more elegant things for the evenings. Smart, simple, easy-to-wear things. The family are on holiday, so you won't need anything too glitzy or glamorous.'

Was that supposed to make her feel better? She sighed, and glanced down at Bambi, noting that she was getting restless. 'Won't Bambi be bored stiff, trailing around after us?'

'We'll buy her some new outfits, too. And, of course, some new toys and books for her birthday. There's a big arcade near the cathedral. We'll find plenty there to amuse her.'

After all, it hadn't been such a bad day. By the time the shops closed for their usual afternoon break, they had finished all their shopping and deposited their purchases back at the hotel.

Sarah found she was even looking forward to wearing her new outfits—the colourful wrap-arounds and tailored separates, the silk shirts and T-shirts, the cotton shorts and trousers, the stylish bathing costumes. And the shoes—the canvas loafers and beautifully crafted sandals. She even had new silky nightwear and fine lacy underwear—Kane insisting, as he pushed her into a lingerie shop, that it was part of their deal.

'You're not worried that you could be turning my head with all this new finery?' she asked archly over lunch. Kane had chosen an outdoor table in the square, where they were enjoying a favourite local dish, *risotto alla milanese*. Milan's elaborate Gothic cathedral, with its intricate rose-white spires and tracery, cast its giant shadow over the square—a magnificent bristling spectacle against the pale blue sky.

'I think your head is fastened in the right place, Sarah,' Kane responded, and a flush seeped into her cheeks, making her wish she hadn't made the flip remark.

'If you blush like that in front of my in-laws, Sarah,' he drawled, 'they will be convinced that we are in love.'

That only made her blush more furiously. 'I'll never carry it off,' she mumbled, unable to look him in the eye.

She bit back a gasp as a steely hand came up to cup her chin, forcing her to look at him.

'Oh, yes, you will, Sarah,' he said, and now there was a hint of menace in his voice. 'Because my daughter's future is at stake, and no matter what you think of me, you do care about her. And this masquerade, remember, is to keep my daughter safe and secure. We're both doing this for *her*. And we'll carry it off, Sarah, between us. We have to. I love my daughter more than anything in this life. For her,' he breathed, 'I'd do anything.'

Sarah's eyelids flickered under his gaze. Yes, she thought. You would. You'd even pretend to be in love with Sarah Vane, a woman who means nothing to you, who you'll never see again after this trip, never be bothered by again. Which is why you chose me. Purely for that reason. Because you know I'm safe and won't cause you any trouble.

Kane's brother-in-law Giorgio, the Corbellis' eldest son, was due to pick them up at three, which gave Sarah, at Kane's insistence, just time to explore the cathedral on her own while he took Bambi back to their hotel for a rest before the drive to Lake Como.

She stood for a moment drinking in the history of Milan in the bas-reliefs on the huge bronze doors, before she stepped into the great Duomo's imposing interior with its massive pillars and stunning stained-glass windows. She felt dwarfed and excited at the same time, the cathedral's remarkable dimensions almost taking her breath away.

'Wow,' she breathed in wonder. 'Wow!' It was all she could say.

'Giorgio, I'd like you to meet Sarah Vane—my fiancée.'

Giorgio's heavy-browed black eyes narrowed as they met hers, but he showed no surprise, Kane having warned the family in advance, as Sarah knew, that he was bringing his fiancée with him.

'How do you do, Giorgio?' She smiled, playing her part.

Kane's brother-in-law, a solidly built, dashing Italian, gave an unintelligible reply before turning back to Kane. 'My family were surprised by your phone call the other night informing us that you intend marrying again... so soon.' He spoke perfect but heavily accented English, the condemnation in his voice barely veiled.

Kane said coolly, 'Nearly two years have passed since my wife died, and that is a long time for a child to be without a mother. I am sure, when you and your family get to know Sarah, you will agree with me that she will make a wonderful mother... and wife.'

Giorgio's heavy brow puckered. 'Is it not... sudden?' An accusing note sharpened his voice. 'When you spoke to my parents previously, you did not even mention that you were bringing someone with you.'

Sarah tensed. Did the family suspect something already?

'Sarah wasn't sure she could get away,' Kane answered smoothly, sliding his arm round Sarah's shoulder. It wasn't, Sarah mused, meant simply as an affectionate gesture, for Giorgio's benefit, but to calm and reassure *her*. But all it did was make her tremble more. 'Sarah's a nurse. Or she was,' Kane went on easily. 'She's given up her job for Bambi's sake. She is devoted to my daughter. As Bambi is to her.' His hand was rubbing up and down Sarah's arm as he spoke, and she wondered if it was a sign that he was feeling as tense as she.

'Shall we go?' Kane's hand finally slid away. He brushed past Giorgio to deposit Bambi in to the back seat of his brother-in-law's shining black Alfa Romeo. 'Sarah, you sit in the back with Bambi, will you? I'll sit up front with Giorgio.'

On the drive north it was Kane who dictated the conversation, enquiring after the family, the European financial scene, the weather, and pointing out things on the way—an orange-tiled rooftop here, a typical Italian farmhouse there, a golden field of corn, a tunnel looming ahead—until they reached the lakeside town of Como, through which they had to pass on their way to the Corbellis' villa on the western banks of the lake.

Sarah was thankful for Kane's easy chatter. It gave her a chance to relax in the seat behind, her hand cushioning Bambi's. With the ordeal ahead it might be her last chance, she reflected ruefully, to relax for some time.

A summer haze hovered over the water. Stunningly blue, the vast lake was indented with timbered promontories. A line of craggy mountains rose behind, their lower slopes peppered with villages.

The road ringing Lake Como was narrow and crowded with cars, trucks and the occasional lumbering bus, but Giorgio drove, Sarah noted with her heart in her mouth, as if he owned the road and felt that all others should give way to him.

For all that, the lakeside drive was breathtakingly beautiful, the road hugging the irregular coastline all the way, winding through small villages and narrow tunnels, past lush gardens and grand lakeside villas, Giorgio jerking a thumb as his car skirted the grandest of them all, the exclusive Grand Hotel Villa D'Este with its sweeping grounds and elegant gardens. The lake lay to their right, the shimmering blue water slashed at times by skimming hydrofoils and chugging ferries.

Finally Giorgio swung the car off the narrow road through a pair of tall wrought-iron gates, coming to a halt on the gravel drive near a big double garage. Below them a terraced garden with curving flowerbeds and stone balustrading descended to the lake's edge. The family's impressive stone villa with its green-painted walls and white shutters loomed over the garden.

Giorgio tooted the horn, bringing a nuggety old man scurrying up the drive to unload the luggage.

As Sarah climbed out of the car and lifted Bambi out after her more footsteps sounded on the gravel. A young, fair-haired woman came running up to them, soft hair flying.

'Bambi! *Cara mia*, you're here at last!'

Sarah tottered sideways as clutching hands tore the startled child from her grasp. Languid green eyes met hers over the top of Bambi's dark head.

'I'm Bambi's aunt, Flavia Corbelli,' the woman said coolly, more to stake her claim, Sarah thought, than with any thought of civility. 'Giorgio's wife.'

Sarah summoned a dazed smile. Whether I'm going to like her or not, she mused, these Italian women sure are beautiful. In her own fair way Flavia—a Botticelli blonde with a swan-like neck and golden skin—was as striking as Kane's wife Claudia.

She felt Kane beside her, his hand closing over her shoulder, gripping rather too tightly.

'Hello, Flavia,' he said. His narrowed eyes weren't on his sister-in-law but on his daughter. 'Bambi, honey, it's all right. It's your Aunt Flavia.' As he spoke he was urging Sarah forward. 'Flavia, I'd like you to meet Sarah...my fiancée.'

Sarah caught a glint of hostility in the green eyes before they snapped away, dismissing her. Only when the woman looked down at Bambi, and smilingly planted a kiss on the child's soft cheek, did her eyes soften. 'Bambi, I am so happy that you are here! I was your mamma's very best friend, do you know that? And you are beautiful—*bella*—just like your mother!'

Sarah could feel Kane stiffening at her side.

'You are frightening her.' In a smooth, quick movement, he extricated his trembling daughter from her aunt's clutches, Bambi thankfully winding her small arms round his neck and burying her face in his shoulder. 'She needs time to get to know you,' Kane said as Flavia's eyes flashed resentment, and it was only then that Sarah noted the jutting chin, the proud nose, the tight-lipped mouth.

It's understandable that Flavia should resent me, and Kane too, she reflected, trying to be fair. Flavia had been Claudia's best friend, as well as her sister-in-law.

Relieving the tension, two young boys burst from the garden, the taller one as dark as the other was fair.

'My sons—Giorgio, who is seven, and Toni, who is five,' Flavia said. 'Bambi's cousins,' she spelt out. 'They have been looking forward to meeting their cousin again,' she told Kane in a honeyed murmur. 'They will love having little Bambi here and will treat her like a sister.' Her eyes flashed for a brief second in Sarah's direction, as if throwing out some kind of challenge.

More footsteps sounded on the gravel, and Sarah saw an older couple approaching, the man silver-haired and imperious, the woman short and stout, with dark red hair immaculately coiffured. Obviously the matriarch and patriarch of the Corbelli family—which Kane confirmed as he greeted them by name.

'Maria, Antonio... How are——'

He got no further as, ignoring Kane, they pounced on their granddaughter, Maria greeting the child in a flood of voluble Italian.

'She doesn't understand you,' Kane said tersely as Bambi cowered away from them, huddling into her father's shoulder. 'Speak English to her, please.'

Flavia snapped from behind, tossing him a look of derision, 'She's half Italian. She should learn the language.'

'Right now she needs to feel secure.' Kane's tone was firm, implacable. 'And she'll feel more secure hearing a language she understands. If she picks up a few words while she's here, that's fine. But I don't want her...' He paused, and Sarah held her breath, half expecting him to say 'brain-washed'.

'Pressured.'

'Bambi... Do you not remember your grand-mother?' Maria Corbelli cooed, her plump tanned hands stroking Bambi's hair, trying in vain to coax a smile from her granddaughter.

'She's very shy... And the long trip has tired and con-fused her,' Kane said, stepping back. 'She needs time to relax and thaw out a bit.'

'If you brought her to visit us more often she wouldn't need thawing out,' Flavia bit out from behind. 'You've kept her away from us for so long she's forgotten us!'

'She hasn't forgotten you. She's just shy,' Kane re-peated, adding impassively, 'Since her mother died it has been best to keep her in a familiar, stable environment. You've always been welcome to come out and visit her in Australia,' he reminded them in the same cool tone.

'Pah!' Flavia gave a snort. 'We all have our commit-ments here, as you well know. We cannot simply dash off to the other side of the world! Australia is... Pah! It is the end of the earth!'

Disregarding her, Kane reached out to catch Sarah's hand. 'Maria, Antonio—my fiancée, Sarah Vane. Sarah, Maria and Antonio Corbelli.' He didn't say my father-in-law or mother-in-law, Sarah noted, as if he was already trying to distance himself from the family.

Dark, hostile eyes pierced Sarah's, neither of her hosts offering words of welcome. Maria swung her gaze away to give Bambi a pat on the arm, causing the child to flinch away.

'Bring my grandchild inside,' the matriarch commanded, dropping her hand. 'Flavia will show you to your rooms.' She stalked off, dragging her husband with her.

'I have given Bambi the room next to mine and Giorgio's,' Flavia told Kane as she led them into the villa through a shady loggia. 'The nursery is presently occupied by Gisela's baby.'

Gisela... Claudia's younger sister, Sarah recalled, who, Kane had told her, had married a professional racing-car driver called Michele. Kane and Claudia had brought Bambi, barely a toddler at the time, to Italy for their wedding.

'And *our* rooms?' Kane asked with a frown, for the moment not interested in Gisela or her baby.

'Your rooms are upstairs,' Flavia said, a glint of something—triumph perhaps?—flaring in her long green eyes as she swept them along a flagstoned corridor lined with wall-hangings and potted plants. 'You will not have to worry about your daughter, Kane,' she assured him, smiling at the child still clinging to his neck. 'I will keep an eye on her. I have been used to getting up in the night, to my boys.'

'Bambi's room is to be next to mine,' Kane rasped. 'And I want Sarah's room on the same floor. Bambi gets nervous at night. And here it is all strange to her. She needs to be close to both of us.'

Flavia's red lips thinned. 'You sound as if you do not trust me—her aunt—to watch over and comfort my own niece!'

'Not at all,' Kane said coolly. 'I am thinking only of my daughter's peace of mind. She likes to be near me. And she has already become extremely reliant on Sarah. Already she looks on her as a mother.'

As Sarah held her breath, Flavia heaved an exasperated sigh and clapped her hands imperiously as the old man who had brought in their luggage emerged from one of the rooms. 'Luigi!' She gave him a string of commands in terse Italian.

'He's to take Bambi's luggage up to the next floor,' Kane translated in a satisfied undertone for Sarah's benefit. 'Into the room opposite mine.'

Flavia tossed Kane a sour look. 'Martha will see to Bambi's room. It is a much smaller room, and has no view over the lake. This way!'

Kane nodded. 'Where's Gisela?' he asked as they headed for the stairs, his tone more conciliatory now that he had got his way.

'Gisela had to drive Michele to the airport. He has a big race coming, so you will not see him. She took the baby with her. Little Gaby is eighteen months old now.' Flavia's voice lost its hard edge as she mentioned the baby. 'Gisela does not often watch her husband race now that she has the baby. I, of course, am more than happy,' she added with a new intensity in her voice, 'to mind little Gaby at any time. I adore little girls.' Her languid eyes flickered yearningly to the child in Kane's arm.

'You're no longer working at the gallery?' Kane asked, neatly changing the subject.

'Oh, yes, I still have the gallery.' With a toss of her head, Flavia flicked back her mane of golden hair. 'I have another partner now...' Her green eyes flashed virulently in Sarah's direction. 'It's closed now, of course, for the summer.'

Pausing near an open doorway, she pinned Sarah with her gaze. 'Kane has told you that he met his wife at the gallery?'

As Sarah hesitated, Kane smoothly answered for her. 'Sarah knows only that I met Claudia in Milan. Flavia and my wife,' he told Sarah impassively, 'were joint owners of the gallery. An exclusive art gallery in central Milan,' he drawled, 'selling art and antiques to those with the money to buy. Is this my room or Sarah's?' he asked abruptly, frowning at the door behind Flavia.

Flavia, still not moving, jerked an impatient shoulder. 'It was love at first sight,' she told Sarah, a glint of malevolence in her eyes. 'Kane had come to Milan on business, to act on behalf of my father-in-law's—and Giorgio's—bank. When Kane met Claudia, that was it. He only had eyes for her. And she for him.' She finished on a note of spiteful elation.

Sarah drew in a long, slow breath. 'I know how deeply Kane loved his wife,' she said evenly, her heart going out to Kane, so silent and stony-faced beside her. Bambi still clung to his neck, mute and wide-eyed.

Flavia moved suddenly, waving red-tipped fingers. 'This is your room,' she told Kane abruptly. 'You will find your luggage inside. When Bambi's room is ready, Martha will come and tell you. Sarah . . . this way.' She left Sarah no choice but to follow. She tossed a smile at Kane as a loving fiancée would, and blew Bambi a kiss as the child peeped up at her from the haven of her father's shoulder.

Flavia led her into a sparsely furnished room with deep-set windows overlooking the lake, the rugged grey-blue mountains making a spectacular backdrop.

'Lovely,' Sarah said, and realised as she said it that she was now alone, quite alone, with Flavia.

# CHAPTER EIGHT

SARAH felt her confidence slip a notch as Claudia's sister-in-law stepped closer, green eyes narrowed, assessing.

'You never knew Claudia?'

Here it comes, Sarah thought. The third degree. She shook her head. 'She died before Kane and I met.'

'How long *have* you known Kane?'

'N-not that long. It's...all happened very quickly.' That's an understatement, Sarah thought, and realised she was trembling. 'Right from the start we seemed to have a lot in common,' she improvised, throwing herself into her role.

'Oh?' Flavia looked her up and down, as if she found it hard to believe they had anything at all in common. 'How did you meet him? You do not look the type of woman who would catch the eye of a man like Kane Brody. Or who would move in his...circles.'

It was meant as an insult, but Sarah, recalling the scathing way Kane had described the women who moved in his circles, felt a cool smile touch her lips.

'No, I'm not from his...circles,' she said quietly. 'I'm a nurse, as a matter of fact,' she said, and remembered to add, 'Or I was.'

'A nurse!' Flavia uttered the word as if Sarah were some loathsome insect that needed squashing underfoot.

'That's right. I'm a qualified paediatric nurse. That's how Kane and I met.' She and Kane had decided between them to be honest about this, though vague about just when they had met. 'I came to his daughter's aid one day when she fell off a swing. I brought her to my hospital for observation and treatment, and came to know them both even better during follow-up visits to their home.'

117

'Bambi needed follow-up visits? How fortunate . . . for you,' Flavia sneered. 'I suppose you are feeling mighty pleased with yourself, landing a—how do you say?—big fish like Kane Brody.'

Sarah forced herself to remain calm. 'I am not marrying Kane Brody for his money, or his position—or for any other *material* reason,' she said coldly.

Flavia eyed her with scorn. 'You are telling me that you love him? That he loves you?'

'That's right.' Kane Brody, come and get me out of this! 'You don't mind if I start unpacking?' Sarah said, turning away to open the suitcase Luigi had dumped on the bed.

Flavia made no offer to help her as she started removing her clothes from her bag and depositing them in drawers, though the sharp green eyes didn't miss the new labels.

'He has taken you shopping already, has he?'

Sarah affected a shrug. 'Silly to buy new clothes in Sydney when I knew I was coming to the fashion centre of the world. I didn't have much time to prepare before we left,' she added truthfully. 'I have only recently resigned from the hospital where I was nursing.'

'Well, why bother to work, now that you have a wealthy man to support you?'

Sarah bit back the retort that rose to her lips. Take care, Sarah, remember the role you're playing. 'Precisely,' she said, thinking, What the hell? Let her think I'm one of Kane's gold-diggers. Let them all think it. It will make it easier for Kane later, when he has to be seen to dump me.

Flavia moved closer, dropping her voice to a honeyed purr. 'Sarah . . . if you love Kane as much as you say you do, you must surely want him all to yourself. You must hate the thought of having to share him.'

'Share him?' Sarah echoed cautiously.

'With his child. *Another woman's* child.'

Sarah tensed. 'I love Bambi. I love her as if she *were*
my own child.' It wasn't difficult to sound as if she meant
it, she realised. Bambi did mean a lot to her—far too
much.

Flavia gave a snort. 'How could you love her? Another
woman's daughter, a *stranger's* child? You are a young
woman, Sarah. You will want children of your own. Why
would you want to bring up another woman's child?
What is Bambi to you?'

Sarah dismissed a painful twinge at the taunting words,
'you will want children of your own', reminding herself
fiercely of the role she was playing and focusing on
Flavia's final question.

'Bambi is the daughter of the man I love!'

She felt something jerk inside her as the words left
her lips. No. *No*, she thought in savage rejection. To
start believing in this role she was playing would be utterly insane—disastrous! *And* illogical, she told herself
brutally. What woman in her right mind would love a
man who looked on all women as insatiable gold-diggers?
And even if she did feel something for Kane Brody, she
couldn't. Falling in love was taboo.

Flavia, so close to her now that she was almost
breathing down her neck, spoke in an urgent undertone,
as if afraid that Kane would walk in at any moment—
which Sarah fervently wished he would.

'Sarah . . . you must think of Bambi, what's best for
her, not what Kane wants.'

'I am thinking of Bambi!' Sarah flung back, reflecting how true that was. She had come to Italy, agreed
to this risky masquerade, for Bambi's sake, not for Kane
Brody's. The child deserved a stable environment, even
if she had no mother to share in it. The child didn't
deserve to suffer the anguish of a tug-of-war between
her mother's Italian family and her Australian-based
father. If this pretence of hers and Kane's could avert
that tug-of-war, she was prepared to bury her own mis-

givings about getting involved and go ahead with it. Wholeheartedly.

'Are you?' Flavia probed. 'Or are you simply thinking of what Kane wants? Sarah, *you* could change his mind. You could persuade him to leave Bambi here, with us. With her mother's family. With her cousins. She belongs here with us.'

'Bambi belongs with her father,' Sarah said fiercely. And just as fiercely believed it. Wifeless he might be, and over-protective, but Kane was a good father, a loving father, and he had the means to provide for his daughter—to provide whatever she needed.

Flavia, realising she was getting nowhere, tried another tack.

'You're very different from Claudia,' she said, with a note of disdain. 'Claudia was so ravishingly beautiful, so vibrantly alive—she lit up a room with her presence. Bambi... She has her mother's eyes and colouring, but her personality, sadly...' She sighed. 'She is a little mouse. So meek and quiet. It is obvious she is unhappy.'

'She's just shy with...' Sarah almost said, with strangers, but realised that would only give Flavia more ammunition to throw at Kane. 'With people. And we have only just arrived here. Give her a day or two to settle down.'

Flavia's lips tightened. 'If she visited her mother's family more often she would not be shy with us. Bambi should stay here, *live* here—Claudia would have wanted it. She wanted to bring Bambi back here many times, but Kane would not permit her to come without him. He is a tyrant. A bully. Since Bambi was born he only brought them here once, very briefly, and he would not let them stay on here without him. Or visit us again without him.'

'Well, it is a long way from Sydney to northern Italy,' Sarah countered. 'A long way for a mother to bring a young child—without the help of her husband. Besides, they were very close, Kane and Claudia. I suppose they didn't want to be apart.'

'Close? Bah! Did *he* tell you that? Claudia was *afraid* of him. She felt suffocated by him. Kane was insanely possessive, jealous—always afraid that some other man would steal her away from him. He wouldn't let her out of his sight!'

Sarah swallowed. Could that be true? Kane had admitted that he had loved his wife... What were the words he had used? To distraction. And Claudia's photograph showed that she had been as ravishingly beautiful as Flavia said. A man *could* be insanely jealous of a woman like that...

'I hope you know what you're getting into, Sarah,' Flavia warned, seizing advantage of her silence. 'Kane can be overbearingly cruel—and brutal. You wait, Sarah. He will rule you with a rod of iron, watch your every move, keep you tied to your home. Claudia wanted to leave him, you know.'

Sarah looked startled. 'She did?'

'Oh yes, but he would not let her go. Kane never loved her—he was obsessed,' she sneered. 'She was his possession!'

'He *did* love her... He's never stopped loving her!' Sarah cried, and realised in dismay that she had used the present tense. 'He *adored* her!' she amended quickly. 'He told me so.'

'A possessive, destructive love,' Flavia scoffed. 'I tell you, Sarah, Kane is a brutal, domineering tyrant. You will find out... if you are foolish enough to go ahead and marry him!'

She swung away at last. 'The children eat at six-thirty, the family around nine,' she told Sarah as she made for the door. 'We have drinks on the terrace at eight-thirty. Join us when you are ready.' She paused at the doorway to make one last impassioned plea. 'Claudia wanted her daughter to be brought up here by her family, should anything ever happen to her. Kane has completely disregarded her wishes. It would be better, far better, for Bambi to remain here with us. She would be with a large family—a close, loving family. She would be secure and well cared for and happy, and given every advantage and opportunity she could possibly need. I would bring her up with my own boys as their sister—Bambi *needs* brothers and sisters.'

Yes, Sarah silently agreed, she does. But she needs her father too, and Kane needs her. Just as Kane needs a wife—a *real* wife. And Bambi needs a mother.

She knew that Kane would expect her to say, '*I* will give her brothers and sisters,' but the false words stuck in her throat and she found herself unable to utter the facile lie. Especially in the light of what Flavia had told her about Kane. Could there be any truth in it? She had seen for herself how overbearing, how repressive he could be.

Flavia, sensing that she was getting through to her, pressed home her point. 'Just as my boys need a sister, and I myself would give anything—*anything*—for a daughter. Sadly——' her green eyes misted over '—I am unable to have any more children of my own.'

On that note, she pivoted round and stalked from the room.

No sooner had her footsteps died away than others sounded on the ceramic tiled passage. Kane stormed into the room, the air pulsating—even more than usual—with his presence, his compelling gaze pinning hers.

'What has she been saying to you?' he rasped, towering over her. 'Injecting her usual poison, no doubt!'

Sarah gulped, and took a step back. 'Where is Bambi?' she hedged.

'I have settled her down for a rest.' He seized her arm in a steely grasp. 'What venom has Flavia been pouring into you?'

'Kane, you're hurting me!'

'Sorry.' He slackened his grip, but not by much. 'Well? What lies has she been telling you?'

'Lies? You're saying that anything she's likely to tell me is a lie?'

'I told you before we came... These people will try anything to keep Bambi here, especially now that they finally have her under their roof. You must tell me, Sarah, so that I know what I'm up against.'

She hesitated, but only for a second. It was only fair to let him give his side. In a few words she related what Flavia had said about him, flinching as he cursed at some intervals and at others savagely dug his fingers into her flesh.

'Sarah, listen to me.' He shook her. 'You have to trust me, you understand? You are not to listen to anything Flavia or the others tell you. Whatever they tell you, you're to put out of your head. You hear me?'

She nodded mutely. She was here to support him, not to judge him. But if none of it was true, why didn't he tell her what the real situation was? Because there *was* some truth in it?

Kane turned his head sharply as footsteps tapped in the passage. They heard a woman's voice, followed by a child's squeal of laughter.

'Someone's coming. No!' Kane's hand tightened on Sarah's as she tried to step away. 'No need for that.' He dragged her into his arms as he spoke. 'We're engaged to be married—remember?'

Just as the footsteps came level with the open doorway his mouth captured hers, his arms crushing her slender softness hard up against his muscular strength. Sarah felt a shudder jolt through her body as her head was forced back by the hungry pressure of his lips, a coil of hot flame licking down her body, dissolving all the strength in her limbs and momentarily blotting out any thought of onlookers.

Kane, with an abruptness that almost made her cry out, tore his lips from hers. She saw a flash of something in his eyes as he drew back his head, and she cringed in dismay. He was mad at himself, obviously, for triggering a response from *her*!

'Sorry if I am interrupting,' said a cool voice from behind.

Kane's head whipped round. 'Gisela! Of course you're not. Come in!' His voice had a husky thickness to it, lacking its usual drawling smoothness.

Damn, damn, damn, Sarah silently berated herself. Now he thinks he's got a complication on his hands, and I can't very well reassure him in front of Gisela!

All she could do was to follow his gaze, and smile numbly as Gisela strolled into the room, a chubby dark-eyed child balanced on her hip. Sarah's eyes widened as she imagined for an instant that she was seeing Kane's wife Claudia in the flesh, but a closer look made her change her mind. There were similarities—the lustrous dark eyes, the mass of black hair, the olive skin, the voluptuous figure—but any likeness ended there. Gisela's features, though striking in their own way, were assembled differently, with less dramatic impact, and she lacked her sister's dazzle.

The child, as dark-eyed as her mother, squawked something in Italian and her mother uttered soothing words. 'She's hungry,' she explained to Kane, making no move to greet him formally, let alone kiss him. But at least, Sarah thought, she wasn't being openly hostile, as Flavia had been. 'Where is Bambi?' Gisela asked, glancing round.

'She's asleep in my room.' Kane was the one who moved forward with a tight smile and proffered his hand, but it was for the child, not his sister-in-law. 'So this is young Gaby. She looks a bundle of mischief.'

'She's a beautiful baby!' Gisela asserted, as if he had insulted her child. Her eyes grew tender as she looked down at her daughter. 'I would like a dozen more like her. And a dozen boys too.'

Sarah bit her lip. Gisela and Flavia certainly doted on their children. The thought brought a sharp pang. She loved children, too, which was why she had trained to be a paediatric nurse, but, sadly, unlike Flavia or Gisela, she would never have children of her own.

'Well, I hope you do,' Kane muttered, the glint in his eyes telling his sister-in-law, As long as one of them is not my daughter! Turning, he introduced Sarah, but Gisela's nod in response was as cool as it was brief. Civil as she might be, Sarah reflected with a sigh, I'll find no ally there.

It was only after Gisela and little Gaby had left them that she turned to Kane and said brusquely, 'I really don't think it's necessary for us to kiss each other blatantly in front of your wife's relatives. Don't you think—in deference to your wife's memory—that a little discretion would be more...considerate? While we're under your in-laws' roof?'

'I thought you quite enjoyed it,' Kane drawled, a mocking glimmer visible beneath the drooping eyelids.

She stiffened, her gaze sliding away from his. 'I couldn't very well slap your face, could I, with Gisela looking on? I just think——'

'OK, you've made your point. Discretion. I bow to your superior judgement. No more blatant kissing.' His tone was bantering. 'You won't object to a brief caress occasionally, I hope, or an affectionate glance...?'

Exasperated, and inwardly raging, in a way she didn't quite understand, she let her gaze swing back to pierce his. 'It's all a game to you, isn't it? Men like you find it easy to play games!'

The teasing light in his eye vanished. 'Believe me, Sarah, this is no game to me. I was simply trying to make it easier for you. Trying to lighten things up a bit. Without wanting you to lose sight of the reason we're doing this in the first place. For my daughter!'

For Bambi... The daughter he'd do anything for, hurt anyone for, sell his soul for. 'I'm not likely to forget,' Sarah growled, stung that he felt the need to remind her. 'But I don't have to like what I'm doing!'

'It might help if you could learn to like *me* a little, Sarah.'

She almost recoiled openly. Learning to like him any more was the last thing that would help! 'Let's keep liking and feelings out of this!' she bit back. 'This is just a job to me. I only took it on for Bambi's sake. Only for her,' she spelt out with heated emphasis.

Only for her? a taunting voice mocked. Did she truly believe that any more?

'Well, it hasn't been too bad, has it, Sarah, so far?' Kane asked her two nights later, as he strolled into her room to fetch her for evening drinks with the family. He had changed from his daytime denims and loose casual shirt into a dark blue shirt that strained across his broad chest, and stylish white trousers that moulded his muscular thighs in a way that brought hot prickles to her skin.

Her eyes flickered warily as he closed the door behind him. Don't panic, stupid. It's only that he doesn't want anyone to hear us.

'It's so peaceful and beautiful here,' she breathed, looking out over the deep blue lake, more to avoid his eye than to take in the view. *He* might not be finding it difficult to act the part of the devoted fiancé, but to her it had been an ordeal having to endure his warm glances and tender caresses these past two days—and, worse, having to respond to them as a loving fiancée would.

'Bambi seems to be enjoying her cousins more now that she's loosened up a bit,' she added over her shoulder. Kane's daughter was still a bit shy with the two boys, but she adored little Gaby, and loved to fuss over the lively toddler. 'I'm glad you brought her back for a visit, Kane.'

And I'm glad you brought me with you, she added to herself, faintly surprised to realise it was true. In other circumstances she would have loved it here on the lake: the sun-drenched days out on the family launch, cruising the lake and visiting the quaint villages along its sprawling shores; the lazy hours spent sunbathing or in the leafy garden watching the children at play; the leisurely lunches in the shade of the columned portico overlooking the lake; the vivid sunsets and long balmy evenings. It was certainly a magical place.

Kane scowled. He, she sensed, was still uptight about being here. About Bambi being here. 'Ready to go?' he asked.

She nodded, and followed him out. The children had already been bathed and fed and settled down for the night, leaving the remainder of the evening stretching uncertainly ahead.

'We won't have to endure Flavia's barbed tongue tonight,' Kane muttered as they reached the stairs. 'She and Giorgio have driven into Como to spend the evening with friends.'

Sarah felt her tense muscles easing at the news. She relaxed even further as the evening wore on. Maria and Antonio, and Gisela in particular, were in high spirits this evening, insisting on opening their finest champagne to celebrate the news that Michele had won a major Grand Prix event that day. They lingered over their *al fresco* dinner out on the terrace, a gentle breeze ruffling the leaves in the trees as they watched the sky turn crimson over the silvery lake.

Just before coffee was served, Sarah slipped upstairs to check on Bambi, reporting to Kane when she came back that she was sleeping like a log. They stayed out on the terrace well into the night, enjoying the delicious coolness of the flower-scented evening. Above them, myriads of stars prickled and danced in the velvet-black sky.

'How about some champagne?' Antonio proposed, just as a telephone shrilled from inside the villa.

Seconds later Lulu, one of the maids, came stumbling out on to the terrace, gabbling something in incomprehensible Italian.

Maria, with a cry of sympathy, translated for the benefit of her house-guests. 'Lulu's husband has just telephoned. Their little girl is very sick. He wants Lulu to come home at once. The doctor is out on another call. Poor Lulu... Of course she must go. She must run all the way.' She waved her hands. 'Lulu! *Presto!*'

'*Run* all the way?' Kane echoed, and Lulu paused, turning her head. 'Where does she live? Can't someone drive her?'

'No need. She lives only a short way up the road. Just round the bend.' Maria waved a dismissive hand. 'Anyway, Giorgio has the car, and Gisela's car has a flat tyre. Luigi has the night off, so cannot fix it until the morning.'

'Lulu will need our help.' A gravelly voice drew the maid's anxious eyes to the silver-haired patriarch of the family. 'She is no doctor,' Antonio muttered.

'I'm a nurse.' Sarah stood up quickly. 'I'll go with her.'

'Oh, would you?' Maria pressed her hands in relief. 'But you speak no Italian. Kane, you must go with her.

Kane hesitated, his brow furrowing, and Sarah knew he would be thinking of Bambi, asleep upstairs.

Gisela was quick to reassure him. 'Do not worry about Bambi, Kane. I will watch over her. I am going up to check on Gaby now. I will check on Bambi too. You had better go... Poor Lulu is getting frantic.'

Lulu, in fact, had already vanished from sight. Grim-lipped, Kane grabbed Sarah's hand and took off after her.

They were grateful there was no traffic about as they clattered along the narrow road. There was no footpath along this section of the road, and only the stars and a narrow crescent moon to light their way. For their own safety they kept close to the low stone wall that ran along the lake side of the road, so that they would be facing any oncoming traffic. There was no protection at all on the other side, just a high stone wall following the curve of the sharply rising hill.

Fortunately Lulu's house was not far, once they had rounded the bend. The high wall gave way to a timbered slope, with the lights from scattered hillside houses visible through the trees. A flight of steep steps led up to the front door of Lulu's small cottage.

Lulu's swarthy young husband met them at the door, and Kane explained in fluent Italian why he and Sarah were there. The young man shifted his feet and muttered something in a gruff tone that brought a frown to Kane's brow.

He translated for Sarah. 'He says his daughter's pain seems to have gone and she has fallen asleep. He's sorry he panicked.'

'I'd still better take a look,' Sarah said, and Kane relayed the message. Lulu nodded and led her to the child's bedside, Kane translating as Sarah asked the husband a couple of brief questions, to which the man shook his head. The little girl barely stirred as Sarah did a quick examination, running her hands over the child's abdomen and checking her pulse and other vital signs.

'There's no sign of tenderness or fever,' she told Kane, 'and they say she's had no nausea or vomiting. I was worried that it might have been appendicitis. Tell them to let her sleep, but to keep an eye on her. It should be safe to wait until the morning before calling the doctor again.'

Five minutes later they were on their way back to the Corbelli villa, this time hugging the sheer curving stone wall, knowing that any cars coming from behind would be on the other side of the road. All the same, they quickened their steps, anxious to get safely round the blind bend.

'There's a car coming,' Kane warned, pulling her closer to the stone wall. 'By the sound of those squealing tyres, the fool is coming far too fast. Let's hope he doesn't cut the corner as he comes round. Crazy Italian drivers!'

Sarah's heart leapt into her mouth. She couldn't believe that anyone would be stupid enough to speed around a blind corner like this one, let alone on the wrong side of the road. 'Aren't they worried about meeting another car on the bend?' she gasped. 'There's barely room for two cars to pass as it is!'

Next second they were both caught in the glare of blazing headlights from behind, and suddenly, as if the driver had caught sight of them at the last moment, there was a hideous screech of tyres. To their horror, instead of pulling up or slowing down, the hurtling car seemed to be out of control.

Sarah screamed, 'It's coming straight at——' The rest was lost as Kane's arm shot out and slammed her back against the wall, knocking her head against the vertical rock. She felt a *whoosh* of air as the car careered past, missing them both by a whisker. If they hadn't both been flattened up against the wall, the car would have knocked them both flying.

The smell of burning tyres hung in the air as Kane spun round and hauled her into the shelter of his arms, crushing her tight. 'Thank God, Sarah! The bloody fool might have killed you!'

She looked up at him, shaken by the raw anguish in his voice. He sounded as if—as if...

'He might have killed you too!' she gulped, and let her head loll against his chest. And I couldn't bear it if anything happened to you, she realised dimly. I care about you, Kane, far more than I should. Far, far more... Deep tremors began to shake her body.

'It's all right, Sarah... You're safe now. It's over.' Kane was dragging her along the road as he spoke, away from the danger of the bend. His voice was unsteady, and she felt another shudder shake her body, not of fear or reaction this time, but some other emotion, hard to define in her shaky state. I do feel safe, she thought, pressing her face into his shirt. I feel as if nothing can touch me, or harm me, as long as I'm here in Kane's arms.

The squealing car, she realised dimly, had screeched to a halt further down the road. Had the driver simply stopped to catch his breath, after finally managing to bring his car under control? Or had he pulled up because he was worried about the fright he must have given *them*?

They heard footsteps running their way.

'I'll murder him!' Kane threatened.

'He could be drunk,' Sarah warned. Surely no sober driver, Italian or not, would drive in that murderous fashion along a road like this. As she raised her head she winced, her hand flying up to press the back of her head.

'Sarah, I've hurt you. Throwing you back against that wall.' Kane's hand brushed her hair, his fingers gently stroking. 'Where does it hurt? Here? Here? What about your back? Your shoulders?'

A sigh whispered from her lips. Anyone would show concern, in the circumstances. She'd be a fool to think he was beginning to care for *her*. He felt responsible for her, that was all, having brought her here to Italy in the first place. To make use of her, she reminded herself brutally. Feelings didn't come into it. They have had, never would.

'Kane, I'm fine.' She was going to have a headache and a painful shoulder, but it could have been so much worse. 'Kane...' She tensed suddenly.

A figure took shape in the gloom. It was a man, shouting at them in Italian. The voice struck Sarah as vaguely familiar.

'He's asking if we're all right,' Kane muttered. 'And what the hell do we think we're doing on the road at this hour of night?' She felt his body stiffen. 'He sounds...'

The driver marched up to them almost belligerently, as if deciding that attack was the best form of defence.

'*Maledizione*! Kane! Sarah! What are *you* two doing here?'

'You!' Kane snarled as Sarah bit back a gasp of recognition.

It was Giorgio!

# CHAPTER NINE

'I TOLD Giorgio to let me drive,' Flavia grumbled, over reviving brandies later at the villa. 'I could see he was in no condition——'

'No harm done,' Giorgio growled. 'See?' He shrugged. 'They are both fine.'

'But they might not have been,' Flavia chided, and Sarah looked at her more closely, surprised at her show of concern. She caught a faint gleam in the green eyes that made her own eyes narrow. She *doesn't* care, she thought with a jolt. It's all a big act. She's sorry we weren't both wiped from the face of the earth!

Glancing across at Kane, she saw that he was frowning, as if he'd had the same thought. She rose from her chair. 'High time I was in bed,' she said, suddenly not wanting to stay in the room a second longer. Besides, her head and shoulders were throbbing and she was still feeling shaky. 'Goodnight, everyone.'

'I'm coming too,' Kane said, stepping over to take her hand. The gesture was meant to be comforting—to show the family looking on that he was concerned for his fiancée—but the soothing warmth of his hand only made her tremble more. 'Goodnight,' he said, with a curt nod to the family.

They left to cluckings of sympathy. Empty sympathy, Sarah thought with a rueful quirk of her lips, voicing the thought aloud as they mounted the stairs.

'More than likely,' Kane said drily. He added slowly, 'Giorgio wasn't as drunk as Flavia made out. He seemed perfectly sober to me. Perfectly capable of controlling a car.'

'Kane, surely you don't think . . .?'

133

'Just an observation.' He didn't speak again until they reached her room. She expected him to say goodnight and take his leave as he normally did, but instead he waved her inside and followed her in, closing the door behind them. She realised she was trembling again.

'The family will think it odd if we never want any time alone together—just the two of us,' Kane drawled, a meaningful gleam in his eye. 'Gisela will be up shortly. Let her think we're—well—doing what one expects lovers to do.'

She panicked. 'But, Kane, I really do want to go to bed. Get some sleep,' she corrected hastily. Why did she feel so nervous? He had a point. As they were an engaged couple supposedly in love, the family would expect them to want to seize any chance they could for some privacy. Kane, of course, wouldn't have come in here for *that* . . .

Why *had* he come in? To talk about their narrow escape?

When he caught her by the shoulders she gave a muffled gasp. 'Kane, what are you——?'

'Sarah, I want you to be careful.' Kane's voice was rough, his eyes fierce under the heavy brows. 'I have an uneasy feeling about tonight. Something like this could happen again.'

'Kane, you can't honestly believe——'

'Think about it,' he grated over her. 'They could have staged tonight's events from start to finish. The phone call from Lulu's husband . . . The so-called sick child . . . The way they cleverly manoeuvred us both to go and help. They knew we'd have to walk back alone together along that narrow road—around that hairy bend . . .'

'Kane, you can't be serious! Giorgio and Flavia were in *Como* for the evening. How could they possibly have known to come along at that precise moment?'

'Didn't you notice that Giorgio has a mobile phone in his car? The family could have called him when we left the villa. Lulu's husband could have called again the moment we left his cottage.'

'Oh, Kane... You're saying that Lulu and her husband——'

'Lulu *works* for the Corbelli family.' Kane's strong fingers jerked her closer, his eyes burning into hers. 'Look, I may be crazy, but we can't ignore the possibility. It's nasty, I admit, but it's what I'd expect of this family.'

She shuddered. 'Kane, it's... I can't believe it!' Was he only saying it to turn her further against the family? To keep her on his side?

'They might not have targeted *you*, Sarah,' he consoled her. 'They would have known I'd be walking on the outside, shielding you from any traffic. With me out of the way,' he said grimly, 'they would have a strong claim on Bambi. With my daughter here in Italy with them, what hope would my mother have? And how hard would she fight?' He showed his frustration by digging his fingers into her shoulder.

'Kane... you're hurting me.' She couldn't think. She didn't know what to think any more.

'Sorry.' His grip slackened. 'Just be careful—all right?'

'Kane, I'm sure you're overreacting. The shock...' It sounded like something out of a chilling movie, not real life. Not real life as she had ever known it. 'But if you're really worried...' She sighed. 'I'll be careful,' she promised. 'You be careful too,' she heard herself warning him. If, heaven forbid, he was right, *he* was the one the family would most want out of the way.

Kane's eyes searched her face. 'So calm! Any other woman would be having hysterics after the close shave we had tonight, let alone at the thought that it might have been deliberate. But here you are, only thinking of me. You're a constant surprise to me, Sarah Vane.' He lifted a hand to brush fine strands of hair from her face. 'How is your head? Your shoulder?'

'Fine,' she said, tensing, more aware of his touch than her throbs and twinges. 'But I *am* ready for some sleep...' Being held in his arms like this, so close that she could feel his body-heat and smell the faint tang of brandy on his breath, acutely aware at the same time of his stroking fingers on her face, was driving her crazy. And the way he was looking at her, that warm shimmer in his eyes... What did it mean?

'Sarah, don't think I don't appreciate what you're doing for me.' The rumbling intensity in his voice set her teeth rattling.

Don't delude yourself into thinking it means anything...

Before she realised what was coming, before she could even draw breath, his mouth was on hers, his arms almost sweeping her off her feet as he pulled her hard up against his powerful body, the heated hunger of his kisses driving out all thought, all fear, all pain. And all sanity.

For a long dizzying moment she gave herself up to the sensations exploding inside her, even openly responding, pressing against him and opening her lips under his, inflamed by the sensual roll of his hips against hers, the intimate touch of his tongue sliding between her teeth, the erotic warmth of his fingers trailing down the slender line of her throat.

The danger they had faced earlier seemed only to heighten the heady wildness engulfing her, a wildness that drove out all her inhibitions, all her protests—for these few mad moments at least.

But when his roaming hand slid over the swell of her breast and began to stroke and knead its soft fullness, sending shafts of piercing pleasure through her, alarm bells rang at last and she dragged herself away from the tantalising web he was weaving, pulling back with a shocked gasp.

'Kane, stop!' She pushed at his chest with the flat of her hands, desperate now to put distance between them. 'What are you doing? There's nobody watching us now!'

She mustn't allow it, mustn't allow what it might end up doing to *her*!

'I know that, Sarah.' He had drawn back, but hadn't let her go, didn't seem to *want* to let her go, his scorching eyes riveted to her face. 'Sarah, you're not to worry. I'll keep you safe.'

She sucked in her breath and snapped her gaze away. Was that why he'd kissed her? Because he was afraid she might turn tail and run off home if he didn't seduce her back into line?

Thank heaven she had pulled back in time, retrieved some sense of pride!

'Stealing kisses behind closed doors was not part of our bargain, Kane,' she said tautly, and heard in dismay the husky plea in her voice.

Inside, tremors were still shaking her body. She had never felt like this before with any other man, had never been so close to losing control—*wanting* to lose control. She had naïvely imagined that she could go through life enjoying the occasional fling, the diversion of an un-complicated affair, but now—now she could see the dangers. At least, with Kane Brody she could. Even if Kane had a brief affair in mind, to while away the tense hours with the Corbelli family, she dared not take the risk, tempting as it might be. Having once had a taste of heaven, how did she know she would have the strength to see it snatched away?

'*Stealing* kisses, Sarah?' A dark eyebrow shot up, mocking her. 'I was under the impression you were giving them freely.'

She flushed. 'It was reaction . . . from our close shave. You caught me at a——'

'Weak moment?'

'Kane, please... Just *go*!' She heard the raw sharpness in her voice but did nothing to soften it. 'I'm tired and I want to go to sleep.' She turned her back on him, stiff-ening her body in rejection, trying to ignore the painful twinges that shot across her shoulders as she moved.

A throbbing silence filled the space between them. Then his voice broke it, his sensual drawl almost proving her undoing.

'Go to bed, Sarah. We have a big day tomorrow, with Bambi's birthday. Sleep well.'

She heard the scrape of his footsteps as he swung round and crossed the room, heard the doorknob turn and the door close behind him.

Only then did she move, letting her breath out in a long, quivering sigh.

'Sarah... May I come in?' Flavia didn't wait for an answer, ambling in as Sarah was pulling on her sandals.

'Am I running late for breakfast?' Sarah asked, glancing hopefully at her watch, wondering uneasily what Flavia wanted. 'If you've come to wish Bambi a happy birthday, she's with Kane in his room. Kane and I have already given her our presents.'

Flavia shook her head, her soft blonde hair caressing her slender neck. 'I will see Bambi when she comes down. We have lots of surprises for her. No...' She swung the door shut behind her. 'I just wanted a word with you, Sarah. About Kane.'

'Flavia, I'd rather you——'

'A word of *warning*,' Flavia cut in. 'I am concerned for you, Sarah. You seem a sweet little thing.' There was a supercilious undertone that she was probably not even aware of.

Sarah's expression didn't change. She wondered what was coming.

'And Kane is a very sophisticated, very worldly man.'

Meaning she wasn't? Meaning she wouldn't be able to cope, wouldn't be able to keep up? 'Flavia, I'd really rather not——'

'Don't expect him to be faithful to you, Sarah.'

'What?'

'He cheated on Claudia, you know... Obsessed as he was by her, much as he made out he loved her. He cannot help himself. He even made a pass at *me* the other night—trying to take up where he left off years ago.'

Startled as she was, Sarah remembered Kane's warning. 'I don't believe it!' she cried.

'You have to trust me,' Kane had said.

'And what do you mean—where he left off years ago?' she demanded, unable to stop herself. Had he chased after Flavia some time in the past?

'You have a lot to learn, Sarah, about your future husband. You think a naïve, ordinary little thing like you can hold him, when he has known women like Claudia—and me?'

'*Known* you?' Her eyes narrowed.

'I had a brief affair with Kane before he met Claudia. Oh, nothing serious—passionate as it was. I am devoted to Giorgio, and he is to me. But we both——' Flavia shrugged '—look the other way from time to time, when one of us wants a little fling.'

Sarah realised she was shaking. It couldn't be true... could it? And why did it matter so much—as much as if Kane really had been cheating? Cheating on *her*? He wasn't. She was just here to play a role. But was it true that he had cheated on his wife—*Claudia*— during their marriage? He was a passionate man, she'd seen evidence of that herself.

'Flavia, I think you had better leave.' She spoke coldly but couldn't hide a faint tremor in her voice. Kane would be proud of me, she thought with heavy irony as misery washed over her. Proud to see her acting her part to the hilt!

Flavia moved to the door. 'I must go down and prepare to greet Bambi.' She drifted off with a smile on her lips.

They had breakfast on the sunny terrace overlooking the lake, the Corbelli family pouncing on Bambi when Kane and Sarah brought her down, showering the child with hugs and kisses and colourfully wrapped presents.

'Happy birthday, Bambi! Happy birthday, *cara mia.*'

Bambi's shy smile widened as, egged on by the family, she started tugging at the ribbons and bright wrappings, revealing an array of elaborate toys, dolls and games. But all the time the child's dark gaze kept sliding curiously to a towering box-shaped gift sitting on the flagstones. It was wrapped in sheets of gold paper and tied with red ribbon.

'Well, now, Bambi...' Flavia's green eyes glinted with excitement. 'Now that you have opened all your other presents, you can open your *special* present—from all of us.'

Sarah noticed that Kane's face was grim, unsmiling. His own presents and hers, already opened before they came down, had been light, easily transportable gifts in comparison with the bulky games and toys the family had given her. As for that enormous gold-wrapped mystery gift—what on earth could it be? And however would they carry it home?

'Here, Bambi...' Flavia grew impatient as Bambi picked laboriously at the elegant layers of gold wrapping. 'I will help you to unwrap it.'

The little girl's eyes widened in wonder as the sheets of gold paper fell away to reveal a magnificent dolls' house—almost a replica of the Corbelli villa, with the same green-painted walls, the same white shutters, the same sharp-angled roof. Each room was decorated and furnished in exquisite detail, even down to the miniature gold clocks on the mantels and the tiny leather-bound books lining the walls of the library.

Bambi's eyes were like saucers. She was struck speechless, her tiny hands stuffed into her mouth.

'Giorgio and Luigi will carry it into the playroom later,' Flavia said, a satisfied gleam in her eyes. 'There is a perfect recess for it there.'

She spoke as if the dolls' house belonged at the villa, as if she expected it to remain there forever. Which, no doubt, Sarah brooded, she and the rest of the Corbellis were hoping it would. And Bambi along with it!

Kane's voice, hard and implacable, intruded. 'I trust the dolls' house and all its pieces—if you wish Bambi to take it home with her—can be packed away for safe travel?'

A heavy silence greeted his question. Flavia shot him a malicious look. It was Maria who finally answered, with an airy wave of her plump hand. 'Anything these days can be safely transported anywhere in the world. In the meantime, the playroom is the place for it.'

Kane, having made his point, said no more. But there was still no trace of a smile on his lips, his mouth a tight line.

The rest of the morning passed in noisy, bustling chaos. The family planned to celebrate Bambi's birthday lunch on board the family launch out on the lake. There was much rushing to and fro between the boat and the house, transporting party food and drinks and extra chairs, Gisela and Flavia staying on board to decorate the boat and the birthday table while Giorgio and Antonio blew up balloons and strung them up on deck.

While all this was going on, Kane and Sarah were given the task of watching over the children, who were playing happily out on the terrace with Bambi's new toys and games.

Shortly after eleven, Gisela, with Gaby's bottle in her hand, hastened out on to the terrace.

'Kane, my mother has a bad headache and has run out of her blood-pressure tablets. Would you mind running Sarah into the village with her prescription? I cannot go—I have to feed Gaby, and the others are all too busy. Mamma also wants a couple of other things while you're at the pharmacy. You are a nurse, Sarah . . . you will know what they are for.'

As Kane's eyes narrowed in quick suspicion, Gisela said quickly, 'I will watch over the children while you are gone. I shall sit down out here to feed Gaby. You will go?' she pleaded. 'Giorgio says to take his car. Luigi has taken mine to the garage for a new tyre.'

Sarah touched Kane's arm. 'Bambi will be fine here, Kane, with the other children and her new games and toys. Everyone else is busy and it won't take long.'

'Please be quick—we want to be out on the lake by midday.' Gisela scooped Gaby up into her arms. 'We do not want to delay the birthday lunch, because after that we have a lovely surprise for Bambi.'

'A surprise?' Kane frowned, and Sarah thought, After last night, who can blame him for being suspicious of surprises?

'Well, I shall tell you if you promise not to say a word to Bambi.' Gisela's husky voice dropped. 'A clown will be coming on board after lunch, and a puppet-show. Bambi will love them, do you not think? The other children will too. It is going to be a wonderful day for them. Kane, you must hurry.'

Sensing that Kane was about to argue, Sarah suggested quickly, 'Bambi might want to come with us.'

'But she is happy playing—look at her.' Gisela nodded to where Bambi was engrossed in a jigsaw puzzle with Flavia's younger son Toni. 'Do not spoil their game.'

'Let her play with her cousins, Kane,' Sarah said quietly. 'We won't be long.' Let him think he was doing it for her, rather than for the Corbellis. 'I'll just tell her where we're going.'

'I'll tell her.' Kane strode over to his daughter, who was meticulously fitting a piece of her jigsaw into its proper place with her tiny fingers. She barely glanced up, barely nodded when he told her he was popping into the village for a few minutes with Sarah.

'Here are Giorgio's car keys,' Gisela thrust them at Sarah, not at Kane, as if afraid he might refuse to take them. 'And here is my mother's list—and some letters she'd like you to post.'

Taking them, Sarah glanced up at Kane. 'Coming, Kane? It won't take us long.'

'It had better not.'

It took longer than they had expected. They used up valuable minutes finding the pharmacy items Maria wanted, and were delayed further by a queue at the tiny post office where they had to buy stamps before they could post the letters. The last straw came when they returned to Giorgio's car and Kane couldn't get it to start.

'Damn! What's wrong with the bloody thing?' After several vain tries, he glanced at his watch. 'Almost twelve already! They'd better wait for us.' If steam could have come out of his head, Sarah thought, it would be coming out now.

'Kane, of course they'll wait for us. Give it another try. You might have flooded it.'

With a fierce scowl he tried again, only to get the same result. He flung himself out of the car, Sarah sliding out of her seat to watch as he raised the hood and leaned over to check the battery and the brake-fluid and then the wiring.

He swore again. 'Here's the problem—a loose connection.' He reached in, fiddling for a moment with the wires. 'Right!' He stepped back and lowered the hood with a bang. 'You'd think Giorgio would check his engine occasionally!'

'The way he drives, it's no wonder things jolt loose,' Sarah said with a rueful smile.

'It's a wonder we even made it as far as the village,' Kane growled. '*Now* let's try it...' Mercifully, this time the engine kicked to life immediately, and within seconds they were on the road back to the villa.

'Just as well you know something about cars,' Sarah said. 'We could have been held up for hours.'

Kane's jaw hardened. 'Maybe that's just what they were hoping.'

'Oh, Kane! That would mean they'd have *known* the car was going to break down. You're not implying——?'

'Let's hope I don't have reason to.' His tone was grating hard. 'They'd better still be there when we get back!'

'Now *you're* driving like an Italian,' Sarah chided as they squealed round a bend.

If Kane heard, he took no notice. 'Damn this traffic!' He swore as a truck blocked his way. 'How long do you think they'll wait for us?' he seethed. Not long, he clearly thought.

'Bambi wouldn't let them leave without us,' Sarah soothed, hoping she was right.

Kane compressed his lips, as if he thought his daughter might not have any choice in the matter.

Luigi had just arrived back with the BMW when Kane skidded the Alfa Romeo to a halt close behind, leaping out almost before it had stopped. Sarah was at his heels as he rushed round the villa to the terrace where they'd left Bambi.

It was deserted.

'Damn them to hell!' Kane's face was thunderous as he burst into the villa ahead of Sarah, to find only the housekeeper there.

'Where is everybody?' he rasped.

The woman stared at him blankly, muttering sullenly, '*Non parlo inglese.*'

With a scowl, Kane repeated the question in terse Italian. The woman gabbled something in reply that drew an even more violent oath from Kane.

'Everyone's gone. Even Maria's gone. So much for her blinding headache!'

Sarah bit back a gasp. 'You mean ... they're down at the boat, waiting for us?' Some hope, she thought. We'd be able to hear them, surely.

'No, damn it, I mean the *boat's* gone! She says they waited as long as they could. Like hell!' Kane ground his teeth. 'They've left instructions for us to take the dinghy out to the boat. I suppose we can be grateful they've left us that!' he added, his tone scathing.

Sarah swallowed. Kane looked ready to blow a fuse, and no wonder. Surely they could have waited a few more minutes?

'If we're quick,' Kane snarled, spinning round, 'we'll make it out there before the birthday lunch gets under way—and before Bambi starts panicking because we're not there!'

That's what's worrying him most, Sarah thought as they both sprinted out into the courtyard. Not missing out on the birthday lunch so much, but that Bambi might be fretting for them... That she might even have been taken out there against her will, causing her added distress.

Or was he fearing something even worse? Her heart quailed. What if the boat wasn't out there at all? It would be her fault if they'd spirited Bambi away somewhere. She had talked Kane into leaving her behind. If anything had happened to his daughter, he would never forgive her. She would never forgive herself!

Clutching Maria's package from the pharmacy, she flew after Kane in the direction of the bluestone-walled enclosure which made a safe haven for the family launch when it wasn't hidden away in the boat-shed. The boat had certainly gone, but to her immense relief a brief scan of the water revealed it sitting out in the middle of the lake, bobbing red balloons just visible on the deck.

She sensed Kane's own relief as he leapt down the steps, making for the small dinghy at the lake's edge.

'I'll board first and check it out,' he shouted over his shoulder, 'before I help you aboard!'

Why would he need to check it out? Sarah wondered, her heart jumping. What was he expecting to find wrong? A hole? Leaking fuel? A useless motor? Did he suspect the Corbellis of deliberately *nobbling* the dinghy? Not that she could altogether blame him if he did, after their close shave last night, and after what had happened just now with Giorgio's car...

As she sprinted down the steps after him something happened that choked the breath in her throat. At the bottom step, Kane's feet suddenly slipped from beneath him and his body became airborne for what seemed an endless second before crashing heavily back, his head striking the edge of the step as he slid into the water, his legs—or his knee, perhaps—striking the side of the dinghy and causing it to rock wildly. Then he sank like a stone below the rippling surface.

# CHAPTER TEN

SARAH screamed. Dropping Maria's package, she leapt down the remaining steps, some sixth sense telling her to avoid the ominously dark patch on the bottom step as she jumped feet-first into the water after him.

Despite the heat of the day, the iciness of the water came as a shock, but she ignored the stinging discomfort as she grabbed out blindly, mercifully finding Kane straight away. She never knew how she managed to drag him to the surface, let alone how she managed to heave him up on to the steps, or his upper half at least, clinging to his legs to stop him from slipping back in.

As he started to cough and splutter, she screeched for Luigi. Where *was* he? Surely he must have heard her scream?

'Kane, you'll be all right!' She had to gasp for air herself, and blink water from her eyes as it streamed from her hair. 'Please don't slip back into the water! I have you—just hold on until Luigi comes!'

And then, mercifully, the old man was there, his callused hands gripping Kane by the shoulders and dragging him higher up the steps, before scrambling back to help Sarah, who was already hauling herself from the water.

'*Grazie*,' Sarah whispered, her teeth by now chattering with cold, despite the warm sun beating down. Flicking back her dripping hair with one hand, she rushed to Kane, reaching him as he heaved himself up on to his elbows, uttering a groan as he raised his head.

His dazed eyes cleared and gradually fastened on hers, taking in her plastered hair, her sodden shirt, her soaked skirt.

'What the hell happened?' He reached up to rub the back of his head, wincing as he touched the tender spot.

147

'You slipped on some oil or grease on the bottom step and ended up in the water.'

'You jumped in after me?'

'Well, I wasn't going to leave you to drown.'

He winced again as he muttered, 'You could have shouted for Luigi. Most women I know would have made *him* jump in after me.'

'There was no time. He did help us both out. Kane, let me see what you've done to yourself...'

'I'll live,' he growled, but his eyes held a tender glint as he reached out to her. 'Thanks, Sarah.'

'Hush. Let me feel...' She ran her fingers gently through his hair, over a lump the size of an egg. When she pulled her hand away there were traces of blood on her fingers.

'Let's get you inside and treat this. You must have a whopping headache... You might even be slightly concussed. Where else does it hurt?'

'Everywhere, at the moment. Nothing serious,' he was quick to add. 'I'll have a few bruises, that's all. Look, we have to get out to that boat. Bambi will be getting frantic, wondering where the hell we are.'

'We'll ask Luigi to take us out when I've made sure you're all right. We'll have to change—we can't go out looking like drowned rats. Bambi will be fine with the family for a bit longer. Kane, can you walk, do you think?'

'Of course I can bloody walk. Luigi!' he bellowed, normality returning to his voice. He rapped out a command in Italian, and then rapped out something else, causing Luigi to bow his head and scuttle off.

'What did you say to him?' Sarah asked curiously as she offered Kane a supporting arm back to the villa.

'I told him to make sure that that grease patch is cleaned off that bottom step and that he's waiting for us by the boat when we come back. I also asked him how the hell that grease came to be there in the first place.'

She looked at him with a quick frown. 'And?'

'He couldn't look me in the eye.' Kane's tone was iron-hard.

'Kane, I suppose he feels responsible...'

'Maybe he *is* responsible. Maybe he was acting under orders.'

Her eyes flew to his. 'Kane, you don't think——' She bit her lip and said sharply, 'Aren't you getting a bit...paranoid?'

'Maybe. Maybe not. You must admit there's a nasty smell about all this. The family bundling us off at the last minute so they can shove off without us. Giorgio's car mysteriously breaking down and delaying us. They'd know we'd be in a hurry to get out to the boat and join them, that I'd rush down those steps...'

'Kane, stop! How could they possibly know that you'd slip and hit your head, let alone end up in the water? Or that *you'd* go down those steps first? *I* could have.'

'They'd expect me to lead the way.' He thrust out his jaw. 'OK, I admit it sounds far-fetched.'

'It sure does. I'll put it down to the bang on your head.' But, secretly, she felt uneasy too. How many more coincidences and close shaves could they expect to have?

'One thing I do know,' Kane said, looking down at her.

'What's that?'

'No other woman ever risked her life for me before.'

'Oh, Kane, I didn't risk my life!'

'Didn't you? You know how deep that lake is?'

'It's deep. I know. About the deepest lake in Europe. But I'm a good swimmer.'

'You could have slipped on that grease patch yourself,' he ground out as they reached the shade of the villa. 'You could have hurt yourself, or hit the boat, or struck something in the water. I could have dragged you under. Anything could have happened. Other women would have thought of that.'

'Obviously I have no imagination.'

He shook his head. 'You only thought of *me*.'

'Well, you were the one in trouble.'

'Sarah, that wouldn't have mattered to a lot of women. A lot of women would have thought only of themselves and their own safety.' He paused under the shady loggia. 'No other woman I've known has ever put me first before—put my safety ahead of hers. Not even Claudia. Least of all Claudia...'

What did he mean by that? She gulped, recalling what Flavia had told her earlier. Hadn't they been as happy as Kane had made out? *Had* Kane cheated on his wife?

She swallowed. 'She did give up her home and her country for you,' she reminded him.

'Yes, because it suited *her*, made *her* happy,' Kane said gruffly. 'I doubt if she was thinking of me—I doubt that she ever really did think of me or what *I* wanted.' His voice had changed, deepening to a low throb, his eyes faintly bemused, as if the thought had never struck him before. 'You've made me aware, Sarah, of how a woman *can* be—how special a woman can be. I've made a lot of mistakes, I realise now, Sarah, where you are concerned.'

'Mistakes? About me?' she echoed, and then wished she hadn't asked. Did she really want to know, really want to hear what he thought of her? Or how special she might have become to him?

'I sought your friendship and made use of your kindness to Bambi, Sarah, because I wanted something from you.' His voice was rough with self-recrimination. 'I offered you money and expensive baubles and other luxuries because I thought that was what all women wanted. All along the line I thought I was offering you as much as you were giving me—or *more*. I was offering you damn-all!' he exploded.

'Kane——' she protested, but that was as far as she got.

'You've asked for nothing, taken advantage of nothing, never thought of yourself, not once. You've only thought of us—of Bambi and me.' He swung her round to face him. 'All other women I've known have cared more for themselves and what they want than for me or anyone else. You, Sarah...' His hands closed on her shoulders. 'You're like a ray of light in comparison. Any man would count himself lucky to find a woman like you.'

'Kane, stop! You don't know what you're saying. It's the bang on your head. It was *Claudia* who was like a ray of light.' She was dismayed at the huskiness in her voice. 'I'm just——' She broke off with a shrug. 'There's nothing remarkable about me at all!'

'That's what *makes* you remarkable, Sarah. The fact that you don't even know it. Your brightness—you don't focus it on yourself. You spread it over everyone around you.'

'There are plenty of women like me,' she cried. 'Finer women by far. You'll find out. Give yourself a chance, Kane.'

'I'd be a damn fool if I let you slip out of my life,' he growled, his hands tightening on her arms.

She felt a flare of panic. 'Kane, we should hurry. Have you forgotten Bambi?'

A shadow darkened his brow. 'You're right...' He stared a moment longer into her face. 'And it's not the bump on my head, Sarah. Unless it's jolted some sense into me.'

As she looked into his eyes shock-waves buffeted her. She tore her gaze away, her throat constricting. No, she thought wildly. *No*!

'L-let's get you patched up and changed,' she mumbled, breaking away from him, 'so that we can get out to Bambi.'

It was less than half an hour later that a taciturn Luigi delivered them safely to the Corbelli launch. As Giorgio helped Sarah up on to the deck, Kane—showing no visible sign of his bruises or the gash on the back of his head—climbed up behind.

'Where's Bambi?' Kane rapped at Giorgio as he climbed over the rail. 'Where is everybody?' he lashed out, his face darkening. Giorgio was the only one on deck.

'They are all down below, enjoying Bambi's birthday lunch.' Giorgio visibly smirked as he answered. 'They could not wait for you any longer. What took you——?'

But Kane was already bolting for the stairs, with Sarah at his heels.

When they burst into the spacious stateroom below the family, to their profound relief, were all there, gathered round a table laden with the remnants of party food. An elaborate birthday cake, already partly demolished, lay in the centre. As Sarah pulled up beside Kane they both spied Bambi at the same moment, the little girl tearing herself from Flavia's clutching hands with a hoarse shriek.

'Daddy! Mummy!' She threw herself at Sarah, sobbing as if her heart would break, clutching tightly as Sarah scooped her up into her arms.

Sarah threw Kane a dismayed look over the child's dark head. *Mummy*, the child had called her. And she had run to her first! She tried to gauge Kane's reaction as he swept them both into a fierce embrace.

'It's all right, honey, we're here now.' He was saying 'we', Sarah told herself, for the family's benefit, stressing that the three of them were a family unit. But no doubt he would have a few crushing words to say to her later, and was already regretting those rash words of praise he'd showered on her earlier—carried away, no doubt, by gratitude and the effect of the bang on his head.

Flavia's sharp voice intruded. 'She's been perfectly all right with us. *Perfectly*. She only started crying when you showed up—she didn't miss you at all. She's been having a wonderful time.'

Sarah and Kane exchanged disbelieving glances. By the look of the child's swollen red-rimmed eyes and the way her small shoulders were shuddering with sobs, she had been crying for some time.

'We're here now, baby, and we won't leave you again,' Kane vowed, a deadly gleam in his eyes as he raked them over the family.

'What kept you, anyway?' Flavia demanded, scorn in her voice. 'We waited and waited... We expected you ages ago.'

'We had no choice but to start without you,' Gisela put in. 'The boat bringing the clowns and puppet-show will be joining us at any moment, and we wanted to have lunch over with. If you want something to eat, you had better grab it now. There's still plenty left.'

Nobody pressed them for a reason for their delay, nobody seemed to care—Giorgio thrusting chilled glasses of champagne at them and Maria, showing no sign now of a headache, bustling round them with plates, urging them to eat.

Bambi clung to Kane's neck while he and Sarah sipped their champagne and picked at the left-overs in a desultory fashion, neither feeling hungry. Kane, determined not to spoil his daughter's birthday, made no mention of what had happened to them, taking Bambi up on deck afterwards to watch the water-skiers and wind-surfers on the lake until the showboat arrived with the puppet-show and the clowns aboard. Their antics drew guffaws of laughter from Flavia's two boys, and from little Gaby, and eventually even coaxed a smile from Bambi too. But she stuck close to Kane and Sarah for the remainder of the afternoon, and not even the other children could prise her away.

'Sarah, I want to talk to you,' Kane said as they left Bambi's room after settling her down for the night.

'Kane, I——'

'*Now*, Sarah. In your room.'

She was hardly breathing by the time he closed the door behind them and waved her to a chair.

'It's time I told you the truth about my marriage,' he said without preamble, his voice hard, without expression.

'The truth?' Her heart gave a jolt. 'You mean—you really did have affairs?' she blurted out.

He stared at her. Then his brow cleared and he gave a harsh laugh. 'Flavia,' he muttered. 'Sarah, I warned you not to listen to her. She'd say anything to drive a wedge between us. They all would. They don't want me to marry again. If they could get rid of me altogether, even better.'

She shivered. 'So what she told me isn't true?' Why was she even asking? It wasn't as if she were his real fiancée. And she never would be. Never *could* be.

'Precisely what has she been telling you, Sarah?'

She looked up at him. 'Did you have an affair with Flavia, Kane, before you met Claudia?'

'Good God . . . never! Is *that* what she's been telling you?'

She believed him. He had no reason to lie about that, surely? It was before he and Claudia had even met.

'She says you made a pass at her the other night.'

'Did she now?' A sardonic smile curled his lip. 'My, she *has* been working on you.'

'Is it true?'

'Hardly. That spiteful bitch? No, it damned well *isn't* true!'

'But you did have other women? I mean . . . while you were married to Claudia.'

'Never!' The denial was swift and violent. 'I never cheated on my wife—sorely tempted as I was at times!'

'So you *were* tempted?' Disappointment pierced her. Much as he had loved his wife, he *had* been tempted.

'Sarah . . . Let me tell you about Claudia. About our marriage.'

As she waited, heart in mouth, Kane started to pace the floor. 'Bambi,' he said, and there was steel in his voice, 'is not to know about this.'

She looked up at him quickly. 'Kane, is it wise to——?'

'Just hear me out,' he grated, and she bit her lip and nodded. 'I loved my wife, make no mistake about that. It was instant—one look and that was it. For both of us. Flavia,' he said drily, 'was right about that. Claudia happily agreed to come back to Australia with me, as my wife.'

Sarah asked tentatively, 'How did she like it—living in Australia?'

'Took to it like a duck to water. I introduced her to everyone I could—friends, colleagues, associates—to give her a chance to make friends.' A rueful note entered his voice. 'She gravitated towards the high-fliers, the socialites, the smart set. Not my cup of tea, most of them, but I tolerated them for her sake, glad to see her happy and popular, making friends so easily. She loved going out. Some of it—the theatre, the concerts, the art shows—were OK, but the rest, the parties, the endless dinners, I could take or leave. Preferably leave.'

'She didn't miss her art gallery, then?' Sarah ventured. 'Didn't want to start up another?'

He gave a humourless smile. 'She preferred to be free. Free to travel and decorate our house and have fun. I was happy to see *her* happy. Happier still when she became pregnant.' His shoulders lifted and fell in a sigh.

Sarah pursed her lips. Why the sigh? She had to ask. 'Didn't Claudia . . . want children?' Was she having too good a time?

'Oh, sure, she wanted the baby. Wanted kids. What true-blooded Italian woman doesn't?' But there was something in his voice now, a bleakness, a brooding note, that hinted at looming trouble.

Sarah hazarded a guess. 'But she didn't want to give up her . . . freedom?'

'She didn't give it up,' Kane said harshly. 'Within weeks of the birth she was back on the social merry-go-round.'

Sarah chewed on her lip. 'That must have been difficult, with a baby to look after.'

Kane's brow plunged. 'She had nannies, housekeepers—I gave her whatever she asked for. She wasn't exactly tied to the house or the baby. I worried about Bambi, but any suggestion that Claudia was neglecting the child and she'd fly into a rage—or else sink into one of her black moods.'

'She suffered often from mood-swings?' Sarah asked, the nurse in her coming out.

Kane's mouth twisted. 'Claudia was always mercurial. Up one minute, down the next. It was part of her charm . . . in the beginning. When she was on a high, she was irresistible. Vital, fascinating, exhilarating.'

Sarah said gently, 'Flavia said she was vibrantly alive . . . that she lit up a room with her presence.'

'When she wanted to . . . Oh yes, she did. She dazzled everyone. Few people saw her less attractive side. The rages, the tantrums, the depressions when she didn't get her own way. The moment she did, she'd soar up again and utterly disarm you.' He heaved a sigh. 'I'd find myself giving in to her, giving her whatever she wanted, hoping it would bring back the charming creature I'd married.' Again that twist of his mouth. 'My wife was a past-master at emotional blackmail.'

Sarah chewed on her lip, a painful memory stirring—and a new understanding of her mother and what she'd been through. She must have felt a similar frustration during her father's long illness.

'Claudia was like a whirlwind . . .' Kane was looking beyond her now, his eyes shadowed, unseeing. 'Always wildly dramatic, always restless for new experiences, always wanting to be the centre of attention. She was an outrageous flirt. I know the men all thought she must be a dynamo in bed. But in private, much as I loved her, our love-life was...' He paused, and she knew he was having difficulty talking about it. 'Unsatisfactory. She seemed incapable of deep feeling. As the months went by she got worse, more erratic, more self-centred, more demanding.'

'People like that can be hard to live with,' Sarah sympathised in the pause that followed. She sensed instinctively that Kane had never opened up like this to anyone before.

'Living with Claudia was like being on an emotional roller-coaster ride that never stopped.' Kane thrust his hands deep into his pockets. 'It was exhausting. After a tantrum *she'd* recover quickly, but I'd be left drained. I told you once, Sarah, that I loved her to distraction. That describes exactly how I felt. Distracted. Frustrated. Helpless. I tried to keep things as calm, as normal as I could for Bambi's sake, but nothing seemed to work.'

Her heart went out to him. 'Kane, you can't blame yourself——'

'*She* did.' A muscle twitched at his jaw. 'In her eyes I was a mean, uncaring tyrant. A bully. She accused me of neglecting her, even when I was only away overnight. When I had to go away for any longer, the scenes when I came home were shattering. I tried to take them both with me whenever I could, but taking a child wasn't always possible. Claudia insisted more and more on coming with me, leaving Bambi at home in the care of nannies.'

Poor Bambi, Sarah thought. She must have felt abandoned, rejected, many times.

'Finally I put my foot down. I could see what it was doing to Bambi.' Kane's face hardened. 'I told Claudia she was to stay at home more, that Bambi needed her. After that she made such a scene whenever I went away without her that I had to cut down on my travelling, though it meant losing contracts as a result.'

'Did that help—having you home more?'

'Nothing helped. Things went from bad to worse. I nearly went mad trying to give her what she wanted—the love, the attention, the understanding, the patience. She was eating me alive, draining the lifeblood from me. It was a nightmare. She destroyed our marriage, our home life, and very nearly destroyed me too. She might have, if she hadn't destroyed herself first.'

Sarah's eyes leapt to his. 'You don't mean . . . she ran her car into that power pole deliberately?'

He gave a shrug. 'She'd made attempts on her life before. Attention-seeking attempts, more than anything. Who knows? The inquest put it down to an accident. She was travelling at high speed when she hit the pole. What nobody knew...' He paused, grimacing. 'Was that she'd stormed out of the house in a fury after I'd refused to take her out to some nightclub when she decided at midnight she wanted to go. I never revealed that at the inquest.'

Deep lines of cynicism gashed his face. 'I wanted the world to believe in the fairy-tale. That we were still happy, still blissfully in love. In actual fact,' he grated, 'I—her devoted husband—could have stopped her leaving the house that night. I didn't.'

'Oh, Kane, you weren't to know what would happen,' Sarah cried. 'You're being far too hard on yourself. Everyone knows how much you loved your wife, how devastated you were when she——'

'Hell, Sarah, don't you understand *yet*?' Kane roared over her, his eyes scorching hard now, his face a mask of bitter self-loathing. 'I was *glad* she was gone. *Glad*! What kind of monster does that make me?'

Sarah's lips parted. So that's what's been eating into you all this time, she thought. Poor Kane.

'A very human one,' she said quietly. 'Kane, it was *relief* you felt. Anyone would. Your torment was over. You're not to blame for what happened. It strikes me you'd tried everything. Claudia had problems, obviously, that nobody could control...' She shivered suddenly.

His eyes slowly focused on hers. 'You have a knack, Sarah, of putting things into perspective. Making a guy feel better.'

'Well, I do know something about uncontrolled behaviour...' Stifling a shudder, she added quickly, 'As a nurse, you often see...' She gave a shrug and let the rest trail off. 'Kane, from what you've told me, Claudia was on a self-destructive path, and nothing you or anyone else could have done would have stopped it. Nobody could ever blame you.'

Except Claudia's own family, perhaps, and how could they know the hell Kane had suffered at his wife's hands? They'd only heard Claudia's side. No wonder Kane had sworn off marriage since! He would hardly want to risk going through that kind of hell again. A lesser man wouldn't have come through it.

'Maybe you're right.' The fire in his eyes had faded, a softer light burning there now. 'Sarah——'

'Kane, you don't have to tell me any——'

He held up a hand. 'I want you to know all of it. You won't hear it from anyone else. Claudia's family have accepted her version—that I'm an unfeeling tyrant who kept her and her daughter away from them. It's true that I wouldn't let Claudia bring Bambi back here to visit them as she wanted to—without me. I didn't dare, knowing how unstable and erratic she was, and that she was perfectly capable of staying here—of leaving me, and never letting me see my daughter again.' He reached up to drag a frustrated hand through his thick hair. 'She'd made threats to that effect often enough, when she didn't get her own way. In her state of mind, I shudder to think what Bambi would have——'

'Kane, you did the right thing,' she heard herself interjecting. Before she could say more he forestalled her, a note of iron hardening his voice.

'I don't want Bambi to know how... bad Claudia got. When I talked to her last week about her mother, I spoke of Claudia as she was when I first met her—as most people saw her. As a dazzling creature, popular, dynamic, exciting to be with. I want Bambi to remember her that way, and not... as she was later. Maybe it's a mercy my wife did leave our daughter with nannies so much. She wasn't exposed so often to Claudia's violent scenes and fits of despair. I'm only thankful that Bambi hasn't inherited her mother's volatile temperament.'

'Kane, it's good that you can talk about Claudia now... and remember her the way she used to be.' Sarah rose at last, her hand reaching out almost of its own volition to touch his arm. No wonder he hadn't been able to talk about her for so long. He must have felt too raw, too full of guilt, too drained by what his wife had done to him... let alone to herself.

Kane caught her hands. 'Sarah, thank you for listening.' His eyes shimmered under his drawn brows. 'Even my mother doesn't know how unstable and irrational Claudia became. She was never exposed to her more violent scenes. Few people were, amazingly. We were seen as the ideal couple.'

He lowered his head and kissed her on the brow, almost reverently. Somehow, that meant more to her than if he had seized her violently and kissed her in the most erotic way.

'I've kept you up far too long,' he said as he drew back.

'Goodnight, Kane.' She smiled up at him. 'Sleep well.'

'I will, Sarah. Thanks to you.'

He turned, and was gone.

Sarah dreamed that she was flailing around in the water, trying to find Kane. Just as she reached him she heard Bambi give a blood-curdling scream, and Kane slipped from her fingers and disappeared. Lungs bursting, she burst to the surface, emerging to the sound of wild sobbing. As she woke with a jolt she realised that the sobbing was real.

'Bambi!' she gasped, and was out of bed like a shot, dragging on her new silk dressing-gown as she stumbled barefoot from the room.

Kane was already there ahead of her, cuddling Bambi in his arms, the child gasping out choked words between sobs. Kane signalled to Sarah to go back to her room and, hiding a twinge of hurt, she obeyed.

But she couldn't get back to sleep. Kane's rejection, the way he had shut her out, had hurt her more than she would ever have thought. But of course... Why *would* he want her in there with them, acting the role of the caring future mother? The Corbelli family weren't looking on now! They were all asleep.

She didn't know how long she lay there staring at the ceiling before she heard Bambi's door being quietly opened and closed and footsteps padding on the tiles. Not back to Kane's room but coming into hers!

She sat up abruptly.

'Sarah... Are you still awake?'

'Yes, Kane. Come in.' She pulled the sheet up to her chin—though she wasn't sure why. The brief costume she wore sunbathing was far more revealing than the lacy nightgown she was wearing now. 'I'll just turn on the bedside lamp.' She flung out a bare arm and switched it on, flooding the bed with its warm glow.

She drew in her breath as Kane, wearing only a pair of shorts, the soft lighting emphasising the muscles of his bare chest and arms, sat down beside her, the bed dipping, creaking under his weight.

'Sarah...' He felt for her hand as it lay on the sheet. 'I waved you out because I wanted to hear what Bambi was saying, and I was afraid she might clam up. You know how shy she can be.'

'That's all right.' She felt a quiver of relief that he hadn't been rejecting her after all. Or was that tiny quiver caused by the touch of his hand in the intimacy of her bed?

'Sarah, she woke up screaming because she'd had a nightmare. It took a while to coax it out of her... I knew *something* was bothering her. The upshot is, Flavia has been saying things to her—alarming things.' The very quietness of his voice was more disquieting than if he'd raved and ranted. 'Like if anything happens to me, Bambi can stay here and live with them.'

'If anything happens to——' Sarah bit back a gasp, her eyes leaping to his, wide with horror.

'Precisely. Flavia told her that she wouldn't be left alone, that *she* would be her mother and Giorgio her father, and Giorgio and Toni her brothers. And that she would live here with them forever and have anything she wanted.' He freed his hand to punch it down on the bed with a vicious swipe that missed Sarah by a millimetre. 'I could throttle Flavia for this!'

Sarah gulped, and nodded. 'Kane... You really think they are trying to—to——'

'We've had two close shaves already,' he sliced over her. 'If they *were* deliberate attempts on my life, who knows what they might try next? And next time they might have more luck!'

Sarah shivered. 'Kane, what are you going to do? They'll only deny it, won't they, if you——?'

'Of course they'll deny it. And be thoroughly indignant and scathing about it. There's no point. Sarah, we're leaving. I want you to pack your things first thing in the morning, and help me pack Bambi's things too—only taking the gifts we can easily carry with us. The family can send out the rest—if they still want her to have them. We're leaving on the first available plane.'

Sarah nodded, chewing on her lip. It was the wise thing to do, of course, but why did she feel so... desolate at the thought of going home, as if a part of her was about to be torn away?

She let her lashes flutter down over her eyes, unwilling to let him see the pain she knew must be there.

They flew up again at the touch of his fingers sliding along her bare arm.

'You've become very precious to me, you know, Sarah. If anything happened to you...' His fingers dug into her flesh.

*Precious* to him? Her lips parted. 'Kane, I——' Any protest died on her lips as his hand moved shiveringly up her neck and got lost in the silky mass of her hair. Why did she feel so weak, so helpless? Why did she long to hear more, to *feel* more? This is wrong, she thought... It can't *be*! But when Kane jerked her into his arms she made no attempt to struggle or pull away.

'You feel it too, don't you, Sarah?' he murmured, burying his lips in her hair. 'The first time I kissed you I felt it. And the second time... And ever since. It jolted me—feeling again, I mean. I knew from the start, I think, that you were different from the others—special...'

He raised his head and looked down at her, at the silky tumble of her hair, the softly parted lips and the wide, vulnerable eyes, his greenish gaze smouldering over the rounded curve of her breast as it rose and fell under the filmy nightgown.

'I'm not going to let you go, Sarah,' he vowed, his fingers tracing the slender line of her shoulder-blade. 'Stay with me... and with Bambi. Give up your plans to work in the outback. If you must go on nursing, find a job close to home—close to *us*.'

She made a muffled sound and shook her head. 'I can't, Kane.' She had to force the words out. 'I—I've made a commitment.'

She felt the warmth of his breath on her face as he brushed his lips over the softness of hers. 'Make a commitment to *me*, Sarah. Stay with me. I never thought I'd say this to any woman, but... I *need* you, Sarah.' His mouth gave a wry twist. 'I've always been the one expected to fill any needs,' he muttered. 'Nobody's ever thought that I might have needs too. You've shown me it's all right to need someone. You've taught me to feel—to trust—to live again. I *need* you, Sarah. I want you with me. With us. Bambi and me.'

She shouldn't listen! Why *was* she? She could feel herself weakening bit by bit, her resolve unravelling. Would it be so wrong to grab at this one chance of happiness—a few weeks, or months, or even a year, if his need for her lasted that long? He wasn't talking in terms of forever. He was asking for a commitment, but he didn't mean a permanent one. He didn't mean marriage. After his experience with Claudia, he'd sworn off marriage for good. Even love didn't necessarily come into it. He just wanted her to be there for him, for Bambi, *now*, while their need was there.

His lips circled her mouth. Tantalisingly, seductively. 'You have needs too, Sarah, aside from your career, though you might not want to admit it...yet. I know you feel something for me. I sense it each time I touch you, kiss you, look into your eyes. Sarah, forget the plans you've made for the outback and stay with me. I want to look after you, protect you, learn even more from you. And Bambi needs you too,' he added coaxingly. 'We both need you.'

She looked up at him helplessly. Dared she? Why shouldn't she give in to her feelings for once and grasp what he was offering...and savour every precious moment? As long as she could be sure she'd be strong enough to turn her back on them both and walk away when the time came...

She gave a tremulous sigh. If she felt she could survive that parting, wouldn't it be worth the pain and the loneliness that would follow? She would always have memories to sustain her in the long years ahead...no matter what happened to her.

'Hell, Sarah, when you look at me like that...'

He groaned, not waiting for her answer, his mouth smothering hers, smothering the last of her arguments at the same time, his arms crushing her against him, so that she could feel the heat of his bare chest burning through the sheer fabric veiling her breasts, bringing the sensitive peaks to tingling hardness against his warm skin.

She felt his instant response, the faint shudder that shook his body, felt him lowering her back on to the soft pillows. Dragging his mouth away from hers, he breathed hoarsely, 'Sarah,' as he grazed his lips across her cheek to her ear-lobe, bringing a moan to her lips as he blew into her ear gently, his hot breath more erotic than she would ever have believed possible. At the same time his hand was roaming over the soft curves of her body—her thighs, her hips, her stomach—each feathery touch making her body tingle and ache for more.

She made a choking sound in her throat as he pulled down the straps of her gown and stroked over the creamy slope of her breast.

'Tell me you want me too, Sarah,' he muttered in her ear, his voice thick with desire as his fingers found the throbbing peak and began a slow, sensual rubbing. 'Say it!' He tore his lips from her ear to trail a line of feverish kisses down her cheek, over her jawline, down into the soft hollow of her throat.

'Kane!' His name burst from her, a throbbing cry of longing. She realised she was clinging to him, exulting in the moist, warm smoothness of his flesh against her breasts, the clench of his muscles under her fingers, the burning touch of his lips on her throat. Did she want him!

As she opened her lips to tell him what he wanted to hear a sound penetrated her euphoria. A child crying, and the scuffle of footsteps. Bambi? No, not Bambi. It was little Gaby down the passage . . . and that must be Gisela running to her. She stirred in Kane's arms, her moan turning to a sigh.

'Kane . . .' Her voice was a husky croak. 'I don't think we should . . . Not here. I think we should wait . . .'

'Until we get home?' He drew back and looked down at her, his eyes smouldering over hers, his breathing ragged, rasping. 'Sarah, you don't know what you're asking! But you're right—damn it. I don't want to make love to you here—not under this roof!'

His hot fingertips touched her cheek. 'When we come together, you and I, I don't want any shadows hanging over us. I want it to be right!' He rolled away from her, his feet hitting the floor with a thud as he swung his legs over the side and sat upright.

'Pleasant dreams, Sarah.' His voice was thick, his eyes burningly tender as he turned and looked down at her. Her lips were still moist from his kisses, her eyes languid under her drooping lashes, her hair spilled out over the pillow in rich chestnut waves. A faint sigh whistled from his lips. 'I need to make a couple of phone calls. One to the airport. And a long-distance call to Sydney.'

His hand brushed teasingly over the swell of her breast as he hauled himself from the bed and strode to the door, leaving her trembling with longing, her nerve-ends screaming for more.

'You're *leaving*?' Flavia shrilled. 'But you can't! You said you would be staying here for a week!'

'I said we would be here for Bambi's fourth birthday,' Kane corrected evenly, 'and that we would try to stay for *about* a week. A full week is impossible now. My agent back in Australia wants us home—he's found a buyer for my house. And he's found another house that he thinks would be ideal for us.' He glanced at Sarah, his eyes cautioning her not to dispute what he was saying or show any surprise.

'You're selling Claudia's beautiful house?' Flavia's green eyes flared in outrage. 'Kane, you can't! My sister-in-law loved that house. She was so proud of it. She turned it into a show-piece. We have all seen photographs—and the spread from *Vogue Living*. Claudia *created* that house!'

'Kane, how could you even think of selling?' Gisela cried, and Maria wailed her own protest in indignant Italian.

'This shows how little you think of your wife!' Flavia sneered at him. 'It will be like trampling on your wife's memory—on everything she did for you!' She turned accusingly to Sarah. 'I suppose this is your idea?'

'Stop!' Kane held up a hand. 'The house is no longer practicable for our needs. It is not a suitable place to bring up a young child. It is, as you say, a show-piece, not a family home. It hangs on the edge of a cliff. There is nowhere for Bambi to play. And it's not safe. The house my agent has found for us appears to fit our needs to perfection. We leave on the midday plane.'

Flavia grabbed his arm, panic in her eyes. 'Why can't you and Sarah fly home by yourselves to look at the house? Leave Bambi here with us? She deserves some time alone with her relatives. Come back for her later!'

'Bambi needs the security of being with us right now.' Kane's tone was implacable. 'She comes with us.'

Amid the howls of protest, Sarah searched Kane's face. Was he really planning to sell his house? Had her comments about its unsuitability swayed him? Or was this all pure fabrication, to give him an excuse to leave?

'I won't buy the house, my darling, unless you give it the go-ahead,' Kane said, a faint gleam in his eye, as if he was secretly enjoying dumping this surprise on her. He pressed home his point. 'It sounds the ideal family home, with plenty of space and rooms, no matter how many brothers and sisters we give Bambi in the future.'

She felt a flare of heat race along her cheekbones. Relax, you fool! He has no intention of getting married again and having more children . . . He's just playing the role he came here to play.

Her chest tightened in a surge of panic. He *couldn't*, could he, be seriously thinking of——?

No! She rejected the thought. Whatever Kane felt for her, however deep it went, it didn't include marriage and

children. Or even love—not *real* love, the kind one expects to last a lifetime. He just wanted her to fill a gap
in his life, and in Bambi's, because they had a need for
her *now*, at this particular time in their lives. If she believed otherwise...

'I suppose you expect Giorgio to drive you to the
airport?' Flavia's sharp voice broke into her fevered
thoughts.

'Not at all,' Kane drawled. 'I have already booked a
taxi.'

'A taxi? Oh, do not be ridiculous!' Flavia snapped.
'You think we would let Claudia's daughter leave in a
*taxi*? Of course Giorgio will drive you to the airport.
We will all want to come and see Bambi off...naturally.'

Kane's eyes flickered at her rapid back-down. 'Thank
you, but no. It is all arranged.'

'You cannot expect all your luggage to fit into one
car!' Flavia's voice rose a notch, edged with faint hys-
teria now. 'We will take both of our cars. Bambi can go
with Maria and Antonio and her cousins in one car, the
rest of us in the other. You cannot deny Bambi this last
chance for some time alone with her grandparents and
cousins!'

Kane's lip curled. He shook his head, his eyes flint-
hard. 'Bambi travels with us. In the taxi. Say your
farewells now, if you please—our cab arrives in
thirty minutes!'

# CHAPTER ELEVEN

'WELL, Sarah, what do you think?' Kane asked.

'Kane, it's a wonderful house. Perfect. It's like one of those homes you see in *Country Life*... There's an inviting old-world charm about it, inside and out. Bambi will love the big rambling garden—and the tennis-court, too, when she's older. And that big rumpus-room will be useful for so many things. Mind you, Hilda will have a lot of rooms to look after...'

'She'll have her own housekeeper's quarters to compensate,' Kane said, his eyes shifting from the house to her. 'You'll have to help me furnish and decorate the place, Sarah. It needs a woman's touch. *Your* touch, Sarah.'

She flushed under the warmth of his gaze. What else precisely, she wondered, aware of a quickening heartbeat, did he have in mind for her? There were plenty of spare rooms in the house... for live-in nannies, for house-guests, for... *his women.*

'I want you to stay with me, Sarah,' he had pleaded with her on that last night in Italy. Stay with him... as what? And for how long? Or did he see things differently now that they were home, now that he was back in his own high-powered world?

They had been back in Australia for two days and so far he hadn't broached the subject. Not that there had been much of a chance. He'd dropped her off at her mother's place after their arrival back in Sydney two nights ago, and advised her to spend the next day recovering from the trip. He would pick her up, he had said, at two o'clock the following afternoon... Friday. Which was today. He wanted her to be with him, he said, when he inspected the house.

Side-stepping his question, she said, 'Bambi loves it too—look at her.' The child was chasing a butterfly along the path ahead of them. 'Did you see the way her eyes lit up when we were strolling round the garden?'

'Mmm... I saw. And I noticed how *your* eyes lit up too, Sarah, when you saw that she'd fallen in love with the place.' Kane's hand brushed her arm, bringing an instant tingling to her skin, even through the soft wool of her sweater. 'You care about her happiness, Sarah, don't you?'

'Well, of course I do.' And yours too, she thought, but felt too shy, too unsure of him still, to say it aloud. Wisest if she never did say it, a warning voice whispered. Wisest if she turned round now and went out of his life forever. But she knew she wasn't going to. Not if he still wanted her to stay. The temptation to succumb to her heart's urging this one time in her life was too strong, overpowering reason and logic. Why not? she thought recklessly. If he wants you to stay... If he asks you again... Why not?

'Sarah, I'm going to tie things up with the agent,' Kane said, his hand rubbing sensuously up and down her arm, weakening her further. 'And tonight we're going to celebrate. Just you and I. Meryl has agreed to come over to babysit. For once you and I are going out alone— just the two of us.'

*Out*? In *public*? She couldn't speak, didn't trust her voice. Dismissing any last lingering doubts, she nodded, smiling.

'Kane, it's been a wonderful evening.' So different, she mused dreamily as he escorted her from his car to her mother's front porch, from their first meal alone together, when he had taken her to Bilson's for lunch. He had chosen Bilson's, not because he wanted her company, not for his own pleasure or hers, but purely to impress her and give him a chance to look her over— and to soften her up for the masquerade he had in mind—in the cynical belief that fine food and wine and a bit of idle flattery thrown in were the simplest ways of turning a woman's head.

How he had changed in the short time she had known him! Tonight he had taken her to a different city restaurant, equally fine in its own way, the cuisine superb, the atmosphere intimate and relaxed, but this time she knew he had chosen the place for their mutual enjoyment, not simply to impress her.

'Oh, I nearly forgot,' she said, diving into her handbag and plucking out a small velvet pouch. 'I should have handed it back to you when we got off the plane the other night, but I didn't think. It's your ring.'

His eyes met hers, a tiny flame kindling in their depths in the amber glow of the porch light. 'I don't want it back, Sarah. I want you to keep it. Here...' Reaching out, he plucked it from the pouch she had put it in for safe-keeping and tried to slip it on her finger.

She snatched back her hand. 'Kane, no! I couldn't. Keep it for...' She hesitated, finding it painful to put into words. 'Kane, even though you might think now that you'll never marry again, one day... You never know...' She gulped, and hastened on. 'Your ring is a family heirloom. It should be kept in your family.'

'I intend to keep it in my family.'

Her head jerked back. 'But you just offered it to——'

'To you. That's right. I certainly wouldn't offer it to anyone else. Ever.'

A heart-numbing suspicion dawned in her mind. 'Kane, what are you saying?' she asked slowly, fearfully. 'Just... what *do* you want from me?'

'You haven't guessed?' He sounded amused. 'Sarah, I don't know what you thought I had in mind when I said I wanted you to stay with me... But I can imagine,' he drawled, 'since I did once tell you I never intended to marry again.'

She froze. 'Kane, what are you——?'

'Yes, I know this must be sudden, my darling. I never intended to rush you. I planned to give you a bit more time to get used to being with me before dropping a formal proposal on you. But, damn it, Sarah, we both know how we feel, we both know we want to be together, and I'm damned if I'm going to let you go on thinking I'm still against ever marrying again when I'm not.' His lips eased into a slow, achingly attractive smile. 'I've changed my mind about marriage, Sarah. You've changed it. You've changed *me*—changed my whole life. Both our lives—Bambi's and mine.'

She gave a strangled moan. 'Kane, no! You don't——'

He silenced her with a finger to her lips. 'Sarah, I know you had other plans for your future, and that marriage wasn't included in them—well, not for some time...'

'Kane, I *never* intend to marry—not ever! I told you that from the beginning, and I—I meant it!'

His eyes didn't even waver as he looked down at her, still confidently smiling. 'I told you the same thing, remember? And I believed it, too, until I fell in love with you and realised I couldn't live without you. You can change your mind too, can't you, Sarah? I won't rush you, I promise... You can have all the time you want.'

She choked back an agonised cry, her mind going into a dizzy nightmarish spiral. This couldn't be happening! It was all her own fault! She had known all along that getting involved with Kane Brody, losing her heart to him, was playing with fire. But she had never dreamed it would go this far, that he would fall in love with *her*, that he would suggest *marriage*.

Kane dragged her roughly into his arms. 'Sarah, just know this. I love you and I want you to be my wife. I want you to be Bambi's mother. She already loves you like a mother. And I want you to be mother to our own children—yours and mine. Bambi *will* have brothers and sisters, just as you always said she should have. Our children, Sarah...' He went still. 'Sarah, what is it?'

She had sagged in his arms, the blood draining from her face.

'Sarah...' He shook her gently. 'Why are you looking at me like that? Don't you *want* children? Is that it?' As she flinched at the question he said slowly, 'No...it's more than that, isn't it? You can't *have* children... Is that what you're trying to tell me?'

She seized on that, and nodded, avoiding his eye. Now, she thought desolately, let that be an end to it. He'll thank me one day for letting him know in time, for giving him the chance to bow out gracefully. As David did.

'Well—that could explain a lot.' His tone was achingly gentle. 'Why you planned to devote your life to your nursing career... Why you specialised in children's nursing... Why marriage was never in your plans.'

She shook herself out of his arms, biting out harshly, 'Isn't it reason enough?'

His hands dropped and he looked down at her. 'Sarah, I don't care if I don't have more children. I want *you*. Just you. Bambi wants you too. We love you. You're our life. We don't need anyone else.'

She gave a tiny whimper. 'Oh, Kane, don't! You just *told* me you wanted more children. Brothers and sisters for Bambi. And so you should...'

'Not if it means I can't have you. If I can't have you, Sarah, I'll never marry again, I swear it. Bambi will be denied the mother she's come to love, and I'll be denied the only woman I'll ever want, ever love.'

She twisted her head away. 'You swore you'd never marry again and you changed your mind. Give yourself time and you'll change it again.'

'Never. Aren't you listening to me, Sarah? I want *you*—only you. What I feel for you is so consuming it's hard to put into words. I thought I loved Claudia as much as it's possible to love any woman. Even with her faults, I loved her despite them, blinded by my passion for her. But even before she destroyed what we had between us there was always something missing, and now I know what it was. You give it to me, Sarah—you make me whole. With you I have the passion *and* much, much more... We *give* each other so much more.'

'Kane, stop! Please!' she croaked. 'There's no more to be said! G-goodbye, Kane!' Flinging herself at the front door, she thrust her key into the lock. She was inside, the door slammed behind her, before he could move to stop her.

It was Sarah's mother who answered Kane's knock— more an imperative thump—at eight-thirty the next morning.

His gaze swept over Laura Vane's trim figure and came to rest on her pale, upturned face. Sarah's generous mouth was there, the same wide-set eyes, the same angular features, but there was a fragility, a tremulousness about her that contrasted with Sarah's calmness and strength, and her eyes held a haunting quality that was absent in her daughter's.

'Mrs Vane, I'm Kane Brody. I've come to see Sarah.'

Laura's slender hand fluttered in the air. 'Mr Brody!' She seemed nervous. 'Sarah...isn't at home.'

'What, at eight-thirty in the morning? You mean she's given orders to tell me that! I saw her car in the garage. Where's her bedroom?' he rasped.

'You can't go in there!' Laura protested.

'Then you go in and bring her out. I'm not leaving without speaking to her. And I'll keep coming here each day until I've convinced her to marry me.'

'M-marry you?' Laura gaped at him. 'You want to *marry* my daughter?'

'I damned well *intend* to marry your daughter! Now...will you fetch her, Mrs Vane, or shall I go and find her?'

'I—I'll fetch her.' Laura made for the door, pulling up with a gasp as she almost collided with Sarah.

'It's all right, Mum. I heard.' Sarah, wearing faded jeans and an old baggy sweater, her face pale and devoid of make-up and her hair in unbrushed disarray, as if she'd had no energy or enthusiasm for either, brushed past her mother. 'Would you mind leaving us for a minute? It shouldn't take long. And then Mr Brody will be leaving.'

'I'll be out the back in the garden, dear.' Laura threw her a baffled look and scuttled off. They heard the back door bang behind her.

'How dare you storm in here and embarrass my mother like that?' Silver-blue sparks flashed from Sarah's eyes. 'I gave you my answer last night, Kane, and I meant it. I won't be changing my mind!'

'No?' Before she could react, Kane hauled her hard up against him. 'If you meant it, how come your heart is racing the way it is? And how come last night when you turned me away your eyes were telling me something else . . . and they still are? How come you're so distressed—if you're so anxious to see the last of me?'

She summoned her ebbing strength. 'Because I . . . Because I'll be sorry to leave Bambi! And because I look on you as a—a good friend, Kane, and I—I'm distressed that you want to be more!'

He laughed, a harsh sound in the neat, sparsely furnished lounge. 'Not very convincing, darling, but a good try! You love me,' he grated, his breath hot on her face, 'and you don't want to leave me any more than I would ever want to leave you! I meant what I said to your mother . . . I'll keep coming here every day until you say yes. I'm not letting you go, Sarah. I only have to look into your eyes to see that you don't *want* to leave me either. You're just thinking of me, as usual. Wanting what's best for me . . . or so you think!'

'It *is* best!' she moaned. 'Best for you, and best for Bambi! Think of *her*, Kane . . . She *needs* brothers and sisters—a proper family life. *You'll* find someone else— someone far more suitable and worthy than I am. You found *me* quickly enough, once you'd managed to let the past go. You fell for me on the rebound!' she accused in desperation.

'Hell's teeth, Sarah, I'd like to shake some sense into you!' He did shake her, his fingers like steel bands cutting into her flesh, shaking until her teeth almost rattled. 'I *am* thinking of Bambi. She'll be heartbroken. She won't understand why you don't come and see her any more.'

'I—I'll come and say goodbye to her...naturally.' When I feel strong enough, she thought. Just now, she felt drained of all fight, all energy, his nearness suffocating her, threatening to melt her will-power, her resolve.

'Sarah, you're going to marry me, and the sooner you realise it the sooner we can get on with our lives!' To press home his point, he grabbed her head in both hands and forced his mouth down on hers, grinding over her lips in savage, sensual demand, his heart thumping against hers, his fingers lost in the tangle of her hair, until, with an animal growl of satisfaction, he felt her lips soften and part under his.

Encouraged, he deepened his kiss, at the same time moving his hips against hers in a slow undulating motion that had a devastating effect on her body, causing her to jack-knife against him, hot flames exploding in a blaze of sparks deep inside her, flooding her limbs with a melting heat.

'We should go somewhere more private... Your bedroom,' Kane breathed raggedly against her lips.

That was what broke the spell, the words 'your bedroom' knifing through her languor and jolting her back to reality. Fighting back from the brink, she tried to twist out of his arms, appalled at her readiness to weaken and respond to his seductive manoeuvering.

'Are you crazy?' she gasped, pretending outrage to hide the weakness that still dragged at her limbs. 'Perhaps you'd like to invite my mother into my bedroom as well! After all, this *is* her house! And she *is* just outside!'

'My, that conjures up a picture. What a droll sense of humour you have, my love.' He was *amused*, damn him! 'I'm learning more about you, my sweet, every day, and loving every new discovery!' His eyes gleamed with relish—and triumph.

Blind, ignorant, misplaced triumph! She gave a deep shuddering moan, more a bleat of pain. 'Well, try this one!' she challenged shakily. 'I'm refusing to marry you, Kane, not because I can't have children, but because I *mustn't*! Ever! Do you understand? And I can't ever marry either! You or any other man!'

'Sarah, what the hell are you talking about? You're saying you're married already? Is that it?'

'No, *no*!' She gave a hysterical laugh. 'If only it were that simple! I could get a divorce!'

'Then what is it?' He frowned at her, showing swift concern. 'You're ill? You have some incurable disease? You think that would make me——?'

'No! It's worse—*much* worse!' She choked back a sob. 'My father had Huntington's disease... And I have a fifty-fifty chance of getting it too—and so do any children I have!' Tears sprang to her eyes. '*Now* do you understand?'

As she tried to break from his grasp, tears spilling down her cheeks, he caught her in a vice-like grip and pulled her back against him, one hand coming up to cradle her head against his chest and brush strands of tear-streaked hair from her face.

'Huntington's disease? You'll have to explain.' He sounded so calm! 'Isn't that some kind of... dementia?' he asked slowly.

'You go mad... yes!' she said brutally. 'You slowly lose your mind, twitching and jerking and losing control of yourself, and then you die! And it can come on at any time. It was destroying my father, bit by agonising bit, until he jumped off the Gap to his death. It could have destroyed my mother too, if his death hadn't spared her any more misery. I could destroy *you*, Kane—and

Bambi too,' she warned, 'if I married you. What your first wife did to you would seem mild by comparison. Do you want that hanging over your future—and Bambi's?'

She had stunned him into silence. But he rallied, and said levelly, 'You might never get it. You have a fifty-fifty chance, you said. Isn't there a test you can take?'

'There are tests, but... I don't think I could bear to know... if they were positive. At least, I wouldn't want to until they found a cure. To *know* it was going to happen would be worse than wondering if it *might* happen one day.'

'All right. We won't have children. We won't take that risk. But you, my darling... That's another matter.' Kane's eyes grew tender. 'We'll put this thing out of our minds and hope it will never happen. If it does, we'll deal with it then. I'll look after you.'

Unbearably touched as she was, she shook her head. 'What about Bambi? You'd risk exposing her? I was lucky—I left home before my father's condition deteriorated to a destructive level. I'd jumped at the chance to get away,' she admitted, flushing. 'It was nothing to do with my father. It was my mother. I loved her but... she was always terribly possessive. Clingy. Over-protective. I felt... stifled at home.'

'So...' Kane's eyes narrowed. 'Your advice to me about not stifling Bambi came from your own experience.'

She nodded. 'I was an only child too, you see. My mother had had several miscarriages before I came along and couldn't have any more babies after me, so I guess that explains why I was so——' she shrugged '—precious to her. Don't get me wrong. I love my mother dearly, but leaving home was the wisest thing I ever did. I learned to become independent and stand on my own two feet.'

Kane gave her arm an understanding squeeze. 'How long did your father suffer before he... took his life?'

'About five years. The first sign was a psychotic episode that landed him in the hospital for a while. After that he developed odd movements in his arms and legs, and later started having seizures—and fits of wild temper. It was hard on my mother, but she coped amazingly well. No one was sure then what was wrong with him. Huntington's was suggested, but he ended his life before being diagnosed. My father must have known... His own father had died of it, though he never told us. I found out later.'

'I guess he wanted to spare you,' Kane suggested. 'Better if you didn't know, perhaps.'

'But I might have unknowingly passed that same risk on to any children I had! Was that fair?' she asked bitterly. 'Luckily for me—or unluckily,' she amended, 'I managed to find out the truth. As a nurse I'd always suspected that was what it could have been. I made a secret visit to my father's family in New Zealand and found out that my grandfather had died of the disease. I've never told my mother. She's always rejected the possibility of Huntington's and insisted that my father was schizophrenic. I suspect she can't face the truth. And as I've always told her I'm not interested in getting married, she hasn't had to worry about me passing it on to my children.'

'So you've kept this knowledge to yourself all this time! Always considering others!' Kane shook his head. 'Well, my love, you can now tell your mother that you've changed your mind about never marrying. And about going into the flying doctor service. Because you *are* going to marry me, Sarah.'

They heard the back door bang as he spoke. Loudly enough to warn them that Laura was coming back inside.

'Kane, I can't marry you!' Sarah cried in despair. 'I can't marry anyone! You know the risk...'

'Sarah!' Laura Vane stood at the doorway, her thin body stiff with shock. 'What are you saying, you can't marry anyone? What risk?'

A sigh hissed from Sarah's lips. She said steadily, stepping closer to her mother, 'The risk of my inheriting the disease my father suffered from. Huntington's disease.'

A spasm crossed her mother's face. 'Dear, your father suffered from schizophrenia. It was *not* Huntington's disease. You have no need to worry. I've always told you there's no danger. I thought you believed me.'

Sarah touched her mother's arm. 'Mum, I found out the truth from my father's family in New Zealand. Mum, I *know*.'

Laura's hand flew to her throat. 'You never told me you'd visited them!'

'Why upset you? You obviously didn't want to face up to it. Mum, I had a *right* to know. I might have inherited the disease! That's why I can't marry Kane or anybody. B-but it's all right,' she assured her mother fiercely, 'I've never wanted to get married. I've never wanted to have children. My nursing career means——'

'You're using your nursing career as a crutch and you know it!' Kane cut in harshly. 'Mrs Vane...' In a stride he closed the gap between them. 'Perhaps you can persuade your daughter that she *can* marry me. Because I'm not letting her out of my life, no matter what happens in the future. Hopefully—and with luck—she will never have to worry.'

'Kane, this is unfair!' Sarah whispered.

'If she ever does show signs of the disease,' Kane pressed on, ignoring her, 'I'll take care of her. I love her, Mrs Vane, and I'm sure she loves me. My daughter Bambi loves her too, as if she were her own mother. We don't need to have children. We already have a child. So, please, Mrs Vane...'

'Call me Laura. Please,' she said weakly.

'Laura... help me to convince your daughter.'

'Sarah, dear, are you listening to Mr Brody?'

'Kane,' he insisted.

Laura flicked him a smile. 'Darling, listen to Kane. He loves you. Can't you see how much? Don't throw away your life, your happiness for no——'

'Mum, Kane's daughter needs brothers and sisters!' Sarah cried over her, her cool control fast slipping away. 'Even if I agreed to marry Kane and we had no children of our own, it still wouldn't be fair to either of them. *I* could still...' She shuddered. 'Kane and Bambi need peace and tranquillity in their lives, Mum, not this terrible threat hanging over their future. They've had enough emotional trauma already. I won't expose them to the risk of having more. That's final!'

Laura gave a yelp of anguish, her hands, shaking uncontrollably, clutching at the air.

'Laura, please don't distress yourself,' Kane said, reaching out to her and steering her to a chair. 'It's *all right* to admit that the possibility is there. Sarah is facing up to it admirably. If it happens we'll face it together. Until that time we'll put it out of our minds. You must, too.'

'But you don't understand!' Laura's lip trembled. 'There *is* no possibility. There *is* no risk.' She buried her face in her hands. 'Oh, Sarah, I feel so ashamed!'

Kane and Sarah glanced at each other.

'Mum, what do you mean?' Sarah dropped to her knees beside her mother. 'What are you saying?'

'I—I never wanted you to know,' Laura mumbled into her trembling hands. 'I was always so afraid that you'd hate me, and never want to see me again.'

'Mum, don't be silly. I'd never hate you. I'd never turn away from you. Tell me!' Sarah urged gently. 'Are you saying...I'm adopted?' She drew in her breath as the implication hit her. 'Mum, if that's what it is, I'll be so relieved! I'll be over the moon! You'll still be my mother... You always will. But I won't have that terrible risk hanging over me!'

Her mother lifted her head, her eyes swimming with tears. 'Oh, darling, it's not that. You're not adopted. You're my own daughter—my only child. But—but...'

'You had an affair with someone else?' Kane suggested from above.

Laura flinched. Gulping, she nodded, unable to look at either of them. 'I've kept it a secret all these years...hoping I'd never have to tell you, Sarah,' she mumbled. 'Even my husband never knew... Jack thought you were his own daughter. He was devastated when he started showing signs of the disease his father had died from. He felt so terribly guilty, thinking he could have passed it on to you, darling. Even knowing how he felt, I—I still couldn't tell him. You know how he could go into rages... I—I just couldn't!'

Sarah felt a wave of sympathy for her mother. 'Mum, did you know when you married Jack that Huntington's disease was in his family?' she asked, thinking of all the miscarriages her mother had suffered before her, Sarah, had come alone. She could so easily have *been* Jack's daughter!

'No.' Laura shook her head. 'Jack's father wasn't diagnosed until after you were born. It came as a terrible shock to Jack. He said we mustn't have any more children, and I agreed with him, so thankful that you, dear—unknown to Jack, of course—weren't in any danger at all.'

Sarah swallowed. 'So... Who was my... real father?' she asked hesitantly, and thought, Does it really matter now?

A flush stained her mother's cheeks. 'He was an American. He...was married too. He'd flown in to Sydney on business. His company and Jack's were affiliated in some way. He dropped in at our home one night to pick up some papers Jack had left for him. Jack had had to rush off overseas—some problem had come up in one of their plants in Saudi Arabia. I invited Ted—

that was his name—to stay for dinner. We got talking and—and...'

'Mum, you don't have to tell me any more,' Sarah said quickly, knowing how every word must be an effort for her mother.

Laura shook her head. 'No. You have a right to know. Ted was a lovely man. A—a happily married man, with children he adored. I was childless, depressed after yet another miscarriage. Ted was sympathetic, and I—I don't know how it happened, it just did. Only that once. I never saw him again, never heard from him again. He... never even knew.'

'Mum... You're sure I was his child and not Jack's?' Sarah asked. She had to be sure!

'Perfectly sure, dear. I was already pregnant by the time Jack got back. I... lied about when you were due. He never guessed you weren't his own child—that you couldn't have been. He was so happy when you were born—he believed me when I told him you were three weeks early—that it blotted out everything. For me too. Ted might never have existed. Jack always looked on you as his own daughter, dear. You *were* his daughter. And he was a good father to you too, until he got sick and... Well, you know how he changed and went downhill.'

'Oh, Mum.' Sarah gave her mother a hug. 'If you only knew how relieved I am! You had no need to feel guilty all these years... But don't let's dwell on that. Let's look ahead!' She rose to her feet and swung round to face Kane, her face shining in a way he had never seen, causing a muscle to twitch at his jaw.

'I've never seen you looking more beautiful,' he said, his hand reaching out to take hers. 'Laura, I'm going to borrow your daughter for a while. Is that all right with you? I might not have her back by lunchtime.'

Laura looked up at him from her chair, too weak with relief to trust her legs just yet. 'You may borrow my daughter for the rest of her life . . . if you would like to. I can see she'll be in the best possible hands.'

'Thank you, Laura. I'm very pleased that you feel that way. When Sarah comes home to you later today, I hope she'll tell you that she wants the same thing I do. No, my darling,' he hushed Sarah, 'not now. With all obstacles now swept away, don't deny me the pleasure of proposing to you again . . . in private. In moments like these, two people should be alone—don't you agree?'

She shivered happily, blushing. 'Let's be alone . . . by all means.'

'Kane, where are we going?' This wasn't the road to his home.

'I want to stop off somewhere. And after that I'm taking you to my mother's.'

'Your mother's? She's back from her trip, then?'

'She is. She's looking after Bambi for the day. I'd like you to meet her.'

'I'd love to meet her too.' Her eyes fluttered to his. 'You're not going to work today?' He seemed in no hurry to rush back to his high-powered corporate existence!

'I'm still on holiday. Besides, I have other priorities than my work these days.'

As he spoke he swung the car off the road into a park, Sarah's eyes widening as he pulled up under a clump of shady gum-trees near some brightly painted yellow playground equipment, the swings and slides and monkey-bars lying idle on this cool weekday morning.

'Kane, this is the playground where——'

'I know. Where you came to my daughter's rescue. Where all of this started. An appropriate spot, I thought, for a proposal.'

Her eyes were a glistening sky-blue as she turned to face him. 'Kane, you're a romantic!'

'You'd better believe it. Come here . . .'

She snuggled up to him, cradling her head in the protective curve of his shoulder. The powerful vibes she had always felt in his presence still electrified the air, even here in his car, arousing all her nerve-ends to quivering life. But now, rather than being afraid, rather than feeling she ought to be running away, she knew she could freely, exultantly give herself up to her emotions, to her need for him, knowing that this was where she belonged, where she would always want to be.

'Sarah... My precious Sarah.' His hand cupped her chin and tilted it upward, his eyes, as tender as they were compelling, reflecting the grey-green of the trees. '*Now* will you marry me? Or, if you feel it's still too soon to be talking marriage, at least tell me you love me and will stay with me... for always.'

She smiled up at him. 'Yes, Kane... Yes,' she said without hesitation. 'To all three. I will marry you. I do love you. And I will stay with you for always. With you and Bambi and—I never thought I'd be able to say this,' she murmured, an almost unbearable happiness piercing through her, 'with any other children we are fortunate enough to have.'

'Oh, we'll have them, my dearest.' He kissed the pulsing hollow at the base of her throat. 'And they will be the luckiest children in the world to have a mother like you.'

'And a father like you.' Her hand strayed upward, threading through the silky thickness of his hair.

'As for me,' Kane said, adjusting his body to hers with a sensuousness that sent a surge of hot blood from her fingertips to her toes, his lips dragging up her throat, across the curve of her jaw to the edge of her mouth, 'I will have the most precious wife a man could ever hope to have.'

As their mouths came together she gave herself freely to the passion of his kiss, responding in a way she had never dared to before, with all the love and sensuality she had kept locked for so long inside, hugging the knowledge that there would be even more exquisite pleasures ahead, and for the rest of their lives.

Above them, exploding into the air like a burst of celebratory balloons, a flock of pink-tipped galahs fluttered from the branches of the gum-trees and flapped noisily into the sky...

# MILLS & BOON

## Next Month's Romances

Each month you can choose from a wide variety of romance with Mills & Boon. Below are the new titles to look out for next month.

| | |
|---|---|
| IN NEED OF A WIFE | Emma Darcy |
| PRINCE OF LIES | Robyn Donald |
| THE ONE AND ONLY | Carole Mortimer |
| CHRIS | Sally Wentworth |
| TO CATCH A PLAYBOY | Elizabeth Duke |
| DANGEROUS DECEIVER | Lindsay Armstrong |
| PROMISE OF PASSION | Natalie Fox |
| DARK PIRATE | Angela Devine |
| HEARTLESS PURSUIT | Jessica Steele |
| PLAYING FOR KEEPS | Rosemary Hammond |
| BLIND OBSESSION | Lee Wilkinson |
| THE RANCHER AND THE REDHEAD | |
| | Rebecca Winters |
| WHO'S HOLDING THE BABY? | Day Leclaire |
| THE BARBARIAN'S BRIDE | Alex Ryder |
| SLEEPING BEAUTY | Jane Donnelly |
| THE REAL McCOY | Patricia Knoll |

# WIN

## A years supply of Mills & Boon romances — absolutely free!

Would you like to win a years supply of heartwarming and passionate romances? Well, you can and they're FREE! All you have to do is complete the word puzzle below and send it to us by 29th February 1996. The first 5 correct entries picked out of the bag after that date will win a years supply of Mills & Boon romances (six books every month—worth over £100). What could be easier?

GMWIMSIN

NNSAUT

ACEHB

EMSMUR

ANCOE

DNSA

RTOISTU

THEOL

ATYCH

NSU

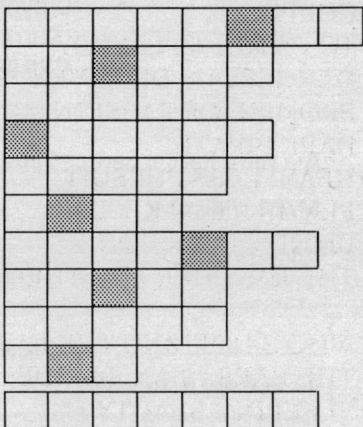

**MYSTERY DESTINATION**

Please turn over for details on how to enter

**How to enter**

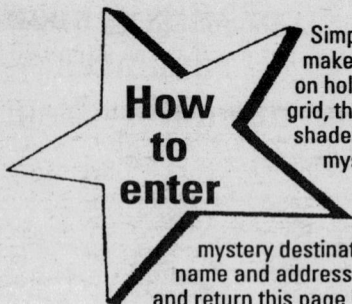

Simply sort out the jumbled letters to make ten words all to do with being on holiday. Enter your answers in the grid, then unscramble the letters in the shaded squares to find out our mystery holiday destination.

After you have completed the word puzzle and found our mystery destination, don't forget to fill in your name and address in the space provided below and return this page in an envelope (you don't need a stamp). Competition ends 29th February 1996.

Mills & Boon Romance Holiday Competition
**FREEPOST**
P.O. Box 344
Croydon
Surrey
CR9 9EL

Are you a Reader Service Subscriber?   Yes ❑   No ❑

Ms/Mrs/Miss/Mr _____

Address _____

_____

_____ Postcode _____

One application per household.

You may be mailed with other offers from other reputable companies as a result of this application. If you would prefer not to receive such offers, please tick box. ❑

COMP495
**B**